VAMPIRE VOW

ISBN: 979-8792604650

Line Editing and Proofing: Jamie from Holmes Edits

Cover: Covers by Juan

Character Art: @kalynne_art on Instagram

Chapter Images: Samaiya Art

CONTENTS

CHAPTER 1

THEY WERE DEAD. I'D FINALLY FOUND MY PEOPLE AND THEY were gone. Burned to ash right before my eyes. I didn't know how I was supposed to process their deaths, or what I was supposed to do once reality set in. All I knew was that the longer we stared at the inferno of Maciah's house, the fewer tears I cried and the more fury I felt.

Sirens sounded in the distance. Given the flames were nearing fifty feet in the air, a neighbor must have called in the fire, but the homes had nothing to worry about. The fire wasn't spreading. It seemed magically contained to the nest. Not even the rose bushes had flames on them.

Maciah snapped out of his rage-filled stupor and muttered something about being right back. It took me a moment to register his words. By the time I did, he was already speeding across the lawn back toward me.

"There is no way in, and the flames are tainted with

dark energy. I can't get to them," he said, voice devoid of emotion.

"They're smart vampires. If there was a way to hide from the fire, they'll have found it," I said. Though, the words felt flat to even me. It was hard to believe even immortal vampires could have survived against the billowing flames and crumbling building.

The fire trucks turned into the driveway, sirens quieting as the brakes squealed.

"Stay right here," Maciah said to me before approaching the first fireman out of the truck. Maciah was probably coming up with some lie that nobody would believe but wouldn't be able to prove otherwise.

At least, that's what I thought until his voice started to rise. "Just look for them!"

I stepped in, bringing my power forward. "Sir, this fire is unique. The firefighters should be extra cautious. There is an unknown chemical fueling the blaze, but you're not going to note that in your report. On paper, this was a gas leak. More importantly, there are still people in the house. If you find them, you're not to call for an ambulance. Just leave them in the yard and be on your way."

His brown eyes glazed over as he nodded. "Yes, ma'am."

I grabbed Maciah's hand, pulling him away so that the men and women could do their job. He took several deep breaths as I held back tears. Speaking so formally about the house and the people inside was painful, but necessary. Screaming at the man to save them would have done nothing. Maciah knew that, but with trembling hands, I knew he was losing control by the second.

"The sun is coming up. We should go," Maciah said gruffly.

"What if they find…" I didn't even know how to finish that sentence. Would there even be anything left other than ash?

"We'll sort that out later." Maciah's ire and grief were rolling off him in tangible waves. His sweet vanilla scent had changed to something darker and mustier. I wanted to make all this better, but there was nothing either of us could do. Not when both of our hearts were shattering.

Maciah didn't show his emotions often. He kept the other vampires at arm's length, but there was a reason those in his nest had stayed for as long as they had. Maciah's actions spoke louder than his words.

I followed him to the SUV we'd driven back from the fight with Silas. Inside were my crossbow and phone, the only two things I still owned besides the tattered clothes on my back. Yeah, that was a trauma to process later. Much later.

All of the firefighters were gathered around as Maciah drove toward the road. The chief we'd spoken to seemed to be relaying the information I'd given, but a few of the others were pushing back. Understandably so, but I could fix that.

"Roll down your window and stop," I said to Maciah. He did as requested, and I leaned across him, directing my energy toward everyone present. "Listen to the chief.

He knows what he's talking about. When you leave here, you'll only remember this was a fire caused by a gas leak with no casualties."

Heads nodded and eyes glazed over for the briefest of seconds. When I settled back into my seat, Maciah drove the vehicle forward. I turned around to stare out the back window, watching the burning house and the sun rising behind us before he turned onto the street.

Fissures formed in my chest, and my throat burned with heavy emotions I wasn't ready to process. On top of my growing grief, I hated that we had to leave because of me. Being unable to withstand the UV rays was a weakness I wasn't okay with. I wanted to be there to watch the flames go out and be the first one to dig through to rubble, searching for any sign that at least one of my friends had not just been murdered.

My nails were digging into my thighs as I thought about having lost all of the vampires. I needed to channel my ire into something productive and stay focused to avoid becoming unhinged.

"Where are we going?" I asked, hoping Maciah's answer would give me something else to focus on for a moment.

"A hotel. We'll shower, get some clothes, and call Eddie. He and Nick need to know what happened." Maciah kept both hands on the wheel as he spoke. His knuckles were white, and everything about him was stiff.

"You're going to have to keep using your mind control to get us in the hotel. Are you okay to do that?" he added.

I nodded. "I'll do whatever we need."

Maciah turned the corner to get on a highway, and the sun came shining through the window. At first, I welcomed its warmth, but then my skin started to itch and Maciah yanked on my arm. "Get in the back!"

Before I scrambled out of the front seat, the itch turned into something I didn't think I'd survive. My blood felt like it was boiling just beneath my skin. Red splotches appeared on my arms and chest, and breathing became nonexistent.

I slammed into the backseat, hoping for relief, but none came.

"There's a blanket in the back. Reach over and grab it to cover yourself," Maciah said, speeding down the highway. There was nowhere to turn off and no point in pulling over. It was better that we got to the next road.

I did as he said, my arms shaking uncontrollably as I barely managed to grasp the wool blanket. I tugged it painfully and slowly over me. The relief was almost instant, but my skin was still heated and itching, so I did my best to stay as still as possible.

"Are you okay?" Maciah asked as I felt the SUV swerve.

"As good as I can be," I answered, my jaw aching from keeping it so tense.

Tears fell down my cheeks from the physical and emotional pain that was coursing through me. I couldn't fathom moving past this loss. Rachel, Nikki, and Zeke had meant so much to both of us. How were we just supposed to move on?

For the first time in years, my initial thought was to just run away. There wasn't a single part of me that wanted to face this grief or continue to deal with the vampires hunting us. I wanted to be done with it all, but I did my best to shut those thoughts down one-by-one.

I'd been strong for seven years for my family, and I'd continue to do so for Maciah's because I'd grown to care about them just as much. Blood wasn't the only tie to a family.

"Almost there," Maciah announced as he made another sharp turn.

I considered peeking out from under the blanket, but I was better off hiding my tear-stained cheeks from Maciah. Instead, I spent the next minute trying to get my crap together for him. The grief was trying to make me weak, but I wouldn't let that happen. The vampires we lost tonight deserved better from me.

I reminded myself that the only way forward was to put one foot in front of the other. The need to curl further into myself couldn't be allowed to grow. Though, the more I tried to push the sorrow away, the darker my thoughts became.

Maybe I was the problem. Maybe I was the reason people around me kept dying before their time. Maybe I was cursed the moment I was born. An heir that shouldn't even exist as a woman. One with too many powers. All this death? It was my penance to pay.

As each thought hit harder than the last, I lost the feeble control I'd been fighting to keep hold of. Sobs grew within me at the thought that I would never be happy. The thought that Maciah would be better off without me. I couldn't stand the idea of staying with him and causing him further hurt, because that was all I'd done since he found me in that alley.

I hadn't heard the SUV stop, but suddenly, I was in Maciah's arms. He was rocking me back and forth, his hands stroking over my sensitive skin.

"I'm so sorry, Amersyn. I don't know how I can make this okay, but I'm going to do whatever it takes to figure out who did this to us," Maciah murmured in my hair as his grip on me tightened. His words were low, and he was breathing hard. A few tears from him fell on my shoulder.

As much as I wanted to push him away for his own good and let the dark thoughts win, I selfishly held on tightly to him, needing his love and strength to get me through this moment. Maciah's touch reminded me of the bond we shared, the magic that had been shared between the two of us when I'd bit him. I couldn't ignore power like that, no matter how maddening my thoughts became.

Maciah was my anchor, and I wasn't ever going to let him go.

We stayed wrapped in each other's arms for an unknown amount of time. We each went through a barrage of emotions, some lasting longer than the previous. With every wave of sorrow, there was never any doubting that Maciah's love for his nest was the kind made for a family.

His palms moved up my arms until he grasped my cheeks, wiping away my tears with the pads of his thumbs. "I love you, Amersyn."

I gripped his shirt, holding on to the black fabric as if my life depended on it. "I love you, too."

Maciah pressed his forehead to mine as we tried to regain our composure. We smelled like death and smoke, and it was time we washed away the nightmare we weren't going to be waking up from anytime soon.

He pulled me from the vehicle, and we were in an underground parking garage of some fancy hotel. There were expensive cars parked all around us and a shiny gold elevator up ahead. Yeah, I'd be messing with as many human minds as it took to get us a room in this ritzy place.

I entered the elevator first and pressed the button for the lobby as Maciah stood next to me. Soft music played that was probably meant to be relaxing, but it grated on my last nerve along with the chime that sounded just before the doors opened.

A man and woman in fur coats were standing in front of the door. The man wrapped a protective arm around who I assumed was his wife, and she put her hands up in the air as if we were pointing guns at her.

We brushed past them, not bothering to convince them we were anything more than whatever their snobby minds had conjured up.

As we continued through the lobby, people stared, gasped, and whispered about our appearance. I didn't blame them. Our clothes had numerous rips in them from weapons and vampire nails. I was sure there was dried blood on my face. Maciah had some on his back where he'd been shot.

By the time we made it to check-in, we'd been called mobsters, hitmen, and contract killers. As Maciah began talking to the concierge, I turned back to the nearest gawking couple and smiled widely, tilting my head down in the creepiest of ways, then waved my fingers at them for good measure.

A woman clutched her pearl necklace and gasped at the sight of me while the man next to her ushered them in the opposite direction. I had no idea why Maciah chose this place. It wasn't somewhere we belonged, not even on a good day.

Though, I smiled softly, thinking Nikki would have enjoyed messing with all these rich pricks as well. Rachel would have been chastising us both to leave the innocent humans alone, even though we weren't actually hurting them.

"I'm sorry, sir. I can't give you a room without a credit card and proper identification," the young man said as his fingers trembled over the keyboard.

Maciah nudged me. "Are you going to help, or are you having too much fun distracting yourself?"

I glared at him, mostly because he was right, but I'd needed that moment of grounding.

I nudged Maciah out of my way and drummed my fingers on the polished wooden surface. After checking the name tag of the young man behind the counter, I smiled at him. His breathing increased causing his pulse to rise and blood to flow faster through his veins.

The sweet scent of honey hit me right in the chest. I took a deep inhale and licked my lips. I was overdue for a feeding, and he smelled delectable.

Maciah's hand rested on my back, and he leaned in close to me. "You're going to give him a heart attack. Get us a room and I will get us food."

I closed my eyes, searching for the will I'd been so hell bent on keeping when I was first turned. I would not kill a human. I wouldn't ever feed from one.

Reopening my eyes, I toned down my psychotic-ness and pushed my compulsion out. "You're going to comp us a suite because of how we were treated when we walked in. We're high-profile clients who require discretion and privacy. We will be here for as long as we'd like. There will be no housekeeping or visitors welcome to our room, which you'll book under Mr. and Mrs. Smith. Do you understand, Paul?"

"We also need clothes. Places like this have personal shoppers," Maciah added to me as the young man nodded.

I sighed. I didn't really want someone else picking out my underwear, but we didn't have much of a choice in the matter.

"You'll also find someone to bring us an outfit each.

Give me paper and pen, so I can write down what we need," I said.

His blue eyes blinked slowly as he reached for what I asked for. "Is that all, Mrs. Smith?"

"Yes, Paul. That's all." I wanted to ask him for blood, but I doubted he could get that on his own without too many questions being asked.

I wrote down the sizes for me and the items I wanted before passing the paper to Maciah. He probably wanted a suit, and I had no idea how those things were sized.

Paul slid two room keys across to us and took the information for our clothes. "I'll get something brought up to you within the hour."

"Thank you, Paul," Maciah said, grabbing my hand and leading us to the elevators.

As soon as we entered, Maciah had to scan our room key before the doors would close. The light for a penthouse floor lit up once the keycard was accepted.

"You did good out there," Maciah said softly, rubbing his thumb over the back of my hand.

"I'm hungry," I replied because it was better than saying how I really felt. Miserable. Dejected. Pissed-the-hell-off. Raging. Murderous. Sorrowful.

I understood how vampires could turn into evil creatures. The grief currently waging a war inside me was too much to handle. Messing with the humans? Wanting to feed from Paul? Those weren't things I would have normally done, not even as a newborn, but they were something that offered a distraction from the mourning. A distraction I so badly wanted. More than anything else.

"Why don't you take a shower, and I'll go see about food. I chose this place because it's close to a blood bank. I shouldn't have any issues getting in and out on my own," Maciah said as we entered the opulent room.

I was on autopilot and hadn't even realized we were inside. I glanced around. It wasn't a hotel room. It was a full-sized house. There was a kitchen to my right, along with a dining area. In front of me, there was a recessed living room with a large sectional and a massive flatscreen hanging on the wall beside the double glass doors that led out to a balcony.

On the left was a hallway, which I assumed led to the bedroom and bathroom. Maciah pressed against my back, guiding me that way. My steps felt heavy as reality once again set in.

Our friends were gone, and they weren't coming back. The nest was demolished. An unknown number of vampires were still hunting us.

How in the world was I supposed to keep fighting?

How was I supposed to keep standing?

CHAPTER 2

WHEN WE ENTERED THE BEDROOM, I WANTED TO FACEPLANT onto the king-sized plush bed, force myself to sleep, and pretend none of this was real.

Except the images of Rachel and Nikki kept flickering in my mind, reminding me I couldn't give up. Damn them for making me care so much about them.

Maciah was right there with me, guiding me toward the bathroom. The room was covered in white tile, and there was a glass shower on our left. He turned the water on for me, then stood in front of me, holding my shoulders firmly. "We're going to figure this out, Amersyn. We're not going to run. We just need to take the day to process what's happened."

Now he sounded like me. The me I was trying and failing to be because the pain was too strong inside my mind. I also knew that as nice as running sounded, I'd regret it later if that was what I asked him to do. I was just having a hard time convincing all my thoughts and emotions to be on the same page.

Maybe tomorrow would be better and I could have the same outlook as Maciah. I tried to speak to him and tell him as much, but the words were too hard and got stuck in my throat.

He stroked my shoulders as if he understood without me having to say anything. "Take a shower. Put on one of those robes in the corner when you're done. I'll be back as soon as I can be."

He kissed my forehead and turned me toward the shower before walking out of the room.

I was surprised he was so eager to leave, but I'd been so immersed in my own woes that I hadn't been paying close enough attention to his. When he got back, I was going to make sure that changed.

I moved robotically as I undressed, avoiding the mirror. I didn't want to see the despair in my eyes or the dried blood I knew was there. My ruined clothes were kicked off to the side, hopefully to never be seen again, and I stepped into the steaming shower.

As the hot water pelted against my sensitive skin, I broke down once again, but I told myself this had to be the last time. I had to be strong enough to fight for my friends. To fight for all of the vampires wrongfully killed.

Without a part of me fighting to stay in control, reckless emotions flooded through me like a tsunami as I thought of Rachel's bright smile, Nikki's strong presence, and Zeke's caring heart. The weight of knowing I'd never see them again brought me to my knees as the sobs tore through me.

I leaned back and slid down the tile wall before wrapping my arms around my legs as I screamed and cried for the vampires that I'd considered family. My throat burned. My chest twisted. My muscles ached. My body recoiled with tremors. There wasn't an inch of me that didn't ache.

This was a nightmare I knew we couldn't make go away, but as the tears continued to pour from me and got lost in the spray of the shower, I promised myself that we'd find a way to make it right. We'd figure out who was responsible and make sure they paid.

As I thought of ways to get the answers we'd need and mentally began making a list of things we could do, my tears stopped. Though, the sorrow never lifted from my heart. As much as I wanted to lose myself inside its darkness, I wouldn't do that. But I also didn't expect the pain to go away anytime soon. I just needed to be strong enough to work with the emotion instead of allowing it to break me.

I pushed myself up from the shower floor and focused on one task at a time. Getting clean was first on the agenda. When that was done, I knew I needed to dry off, brush my hair, wear the robe, and wait for Maciah.

Each task took little to no effort and they were done much too quickly. As I tightened the robe around me, not knowing what to do next, the sense of loss began to creep back in. What was I supposed to do while I waited for

Maciah? What would I have done before when I was on my own?

Research. That's what. I still had my phone. It was in the back pocket of the pants I'd kicked to the corner of the bathroom. I shook out my clothes until I felt the phone and cursed when I saw the battery was at sixteen percent.

This was a ritzy hotel, though. If there wasn't a charger in the room, I had a feeling the front desk would be more than happy to bring me one.

I began opening the drawers in the closet, but it wasn't until I got to the nightstand that I found what I needed. Plugging in the USB first, I stretched the cord across the bed and piled pillows behind me before getting comfortable. I didn't know how long Maciah was going to be gone, but I wouldn't rest for a moment until I had a solid plan for us.

With my phone charging, I pulled up the hunter app. I wasn't sure how much would be there with Simon playing a role in some of the things happening around us, but if anyone knew something and wanted to put a warning out, this was where I'd find it.

I scrolled through the posts, skimming the keywords of each recent post looking for anything about Simon, Viktor, Silas, and even myself.

There was no telling what information had been passed along about what I'd become. Hunters wouldn't understand. They'd assume I chose this life, but even though I didn't put up much of a fight once I got to know the vampires around me, I never would have voluntarily become one.

I loved Maciah and would have spent as much of my life with him as I could have, but giving up my human existence without being forced wasn't something I would have done. At least, not in the short term. Maybe I'd have grown to change my mind, but the old me that still lived in the far recesses of my mind didn't think so. She was stubborn, sometimes to a fault.

Before I could find anything helpful in the app, Maciah's voice sounded in the hallway. I slid off the bed and went to the door as he opened it, phone held between his cheek and shoulder since his hands were full of bags.

I took the items from his hands, and he grabbed the phone, putting it on speaker.

Eddie's voice sounded. "The doctors said everything went well. The wounds he sustained were mostly to his ribs, and Dave was likely only unconscious for so long due to self-preservation."

I'd almost forgotten about my bartender with everything else going on. Hearing the update lifted my spirits slightly, but poor Dave. I'd have hidden from the reality of vampires beating the hell out of me, too, if I was him.

"Thank you, Eddie. I don't know what we're doing, but I have a room here for you guys until we figure it out," Maciah said, then gestured to me. "Anything you want to ask?"

I stepped closer to the phone. "Did Dave wake up yet?"

"No, but that's because the doctors don't want him awake yet. They said he should be up tonight, as long as things keep progressing as they have been. We'll stay until he does or until you guys need us, whichever comes first," Eddie answered.

"Thank you for staying with him," I said.

"I'm glad I did." Eddie ended the call, and I shuddered. I bet he was. If Eddie and Nick had gone back to the mansion, they'd likely be dead.

Maciah took one of the bags from me and pulled out a cooler. My mouth immediately began to salivate, and my fangs were begging to be set free. I had done a good job of distracting myself from the hunger, but knowing there was blood so close that I could have without hurting anyone…

Famished. Ravenous. Starved to near death. Each one more dramatic than the other, but I couldn't stop the thoughts from circling my mind.

Maciah gave me the first blood bag, and I opened it before he could pull out another. I didn't know anything about the blood bank where he'd taken these from, but as long as they were donated, I had no time to ask questions.

The fight with Silas had taken a lot of energy and the grief that followed was more than any vampire should have had to handle. As the crimson liquid slid down my throat, it soothed the frayed ends of my nerves, but there was no amount I could drink that would stitch my heart back together.

I drank one more bag before deciding I needed to slow down, then began to rummage through the other two bags. There was a suit in one and women's clothes in the other.

"Did you get these from the front desk?" I asked as I pulled out the clothes.

Maciah shook his head. "I told him I'd grab something while I was out once I realized there was a store across the street.

I slid the underwear on first before wiggling into the jeans. They were a bit smaller than I expected for the size, but they'd work. The green top, however, was the softest cotton I'd ever felt, and there was a leather jacket at the bottom of the bag.

"How did you get all of this from the store? Did they let you charge it to the room?" I asked as I sat back down on the bed.

"I went to the bank first, and they printed me a new credit card," he said, putting the rest of the blood into the fridge of the hotel room.

"They can do that?" I was a little surprised at that.

He nodded. "They have a copy of my ID on file, so it really wasn't a big deal. I just told them my wallet was stolen."

I raised a brow, appraising him. "Did they question your attire?"

"Nope." He gave me a small smirk and I rolled my

eyes. His perfectly handsome face was probably all the poor tellers saw the moment he walked in.

"So, I was thinking. There isn't anything on the hunter app about Simon, which tells me he's likely fully immersed in the vampire world now. We should head to LA and regroup. See what kind of help we can find there," I said as I hopped onto the counter.

I'd considered suggesting that we go to my old condo. I was pretty sure the windows had been fixed by insurance, and I knew Rachel and Nikki had cleaned the place up the one night they'd stayed there, but my gut told me we weren't going to find what we needed here. Not anymore.

Maciah grabbed his bag that I'd left at the foot of the bed. His hands shook so slightly that someone not paying attention would have missed it. There was a twitch in his cheek, and his eyes were darker than normal even though he'd just fed.

He nodded at my suggestion of going to LA but stayed silent. I slid off the bed and went to him, forcing him to sit on the edge of the mattress.

I twisted so that I was sitting sideways and facing him, then grabbed his hand. "Talk to me."

"About what?"

Men. I wanted to roll my eyes but managed to refrain. "Don't hold this in, Maciah. It will only make things worse when you explode later. We need to be on the same page and that includes how we're feeling."

"I'm fine," he insisted.

"No, you're not. If you were, I'd actually be more concerned, but you can't hide how badly you're hurting from me, no matter how hard you try. I saw a glimpse of it in the car, and you shouldn't be afraid to tell me what you're thinking."

He sighed. "I'm not afraid, but there's no point. I have a job to do and how I feel can't affect that."

Something must have happened before I came along, something within his nest that had hardened him. I'd always noticed that Maciah didn't get as friendly with the other vampires as they were with each other, but I'd never thought too hard about it. As a leader, I could imagine there was a fine line between being friends with the vampires he was charged to protect and making sure none of them abused that friendship.

And because I couldn't let this go, I kept pressing him. "What happened, Maciah? Your nest clearly cared for you and there was a reason for that. Besides the fact that you kept them safe or saved them from a life they never wanted."

He pulled his hand from my hold and rubbed his palms over his face. "It doesn't matter."

"Yes, it does."

Maciah met my stare and his face softened. "You're not going to let this go, are you?"

"It's not likely," I said, trying to be sensitive yet persistent. Maciah needed this, and I was going to make him see that. I just didn't know what was inside his head.

"I used to run the nest differently. We threw parties,

did things together, and kept each other company when there was nothing else to do. I made friends with the vampires, but some took advantage of that friendship and thought they could do things in my nest that I didn't stand for. So, I stopped the parties, changed having so many vampires stay in the rooms inside the main house, and created boundaries."

That was pretty much what I assumed, but I knew there was something more.

"Did that help?" I asked.

"For a while. I kept a few vampires close to me, Zeke and Bennett being the ones I trusted most. Then, Bennett left without a word as to where he was going or if he'd be back. I'd relied on him, and then he was gone."

I hadn't thought how Bennett's departure from the nest would have made anyone else feel other than Nikki since they'd been in a relationship. I couldn't believe nobody had mentioned this to me before.

"I'm sorry you had to go through that," I said, unsure what else I could say or do.

"I knew then that I couldn't be friends with any of them—not the way I was before—if I was going to accomplish the things I'd set out to do in the beginning. I kept Zeke and Rachel closest, needing at least a couple people I could trust at my side. Even still, they never saw beyond what I wanted them to once my decision was made. I don't even know why any of them stayed once I changed. There were more rules and less fun within the nest, and I didn't apologize once for my actions," he said, voice filled with a vulnerability I'd never heard from him.

I leaned against his shoulder. "They stayed because it doesn't matter if you stopped talking to the vampires or showing them your emotions. It's your actions that speak loudest. You never stopped trying to give them a life they didn't hate."

His head leaned onto mine. "Maybe."

"There's no *maybe* about it. You were exactly what they needed."

He scoffed. "Until I got them all killed."

"The fire wasn't your fault. Don't blame yourself for that. I know none of them would."

A shudder rolled through Maciah before he began to harden back into the leader he strived to be. "We have to find who sent the drones."

I sighed, knowing he wasn't going to agree with me about where the blame lay, and I could tell he was done sharing by the tense set in his shoulders. Instead of continuing to push him, I leaned up and asked, "What do you think about my idea of going to LA?"

"We can't consider leaving the hotel until nightfall. Even though more people know where the LA house is than any other, I agree. We have more resources there than any of the other places we could go."

I'd forgotten Maciah had multiple homes. Maybe he wasn't thinking about all of the resources, though. "Do you have one near the wolves or other vampire nests?"

He shook his head. "I try to keep them private, but I

can see maybe I need to invest in some more real estate now."

"That's something to think about later. Since we can't go anywhere until sunset, thanks to me, why don't you go take a shower? I'll keep searching the internet for anything that might be helpful. It's amazing what you can find there when you know what you're looking for," I said, remembering how I'd found the group of hunters when I was only a teenager.

Maciah stood and brought me up with him before holding my face gently between his hands and pressing his lips to my forehead. "Thank you."

"Just remember none of this is your fault and you're welcome," I whispered as our grief intertwined.

"I'm trying, but I should have known Silas would have contingencies. I should have moved the entire nest. Instead, they did what they always do when we get done with a mission like this. Every vampire was gathered in the mansion, waiting for us to get home, and now they're all dead because of it. Now, you're hurting from having lost more people you care about. All because I didn't think ahead."

My hands covered his. "You are not a murdering vampire. There is no possible way you could have predicted something like what happened. You are not Silas, and it would have worried me more if you'd been able to think like him."

I pushed up onto my toes and pressed my lips to his. "We're going to figure this out. Together. We're going to get the vengeance every single one of those vampires deserves. Then, we're going to kill Viktor so we can properly take an extended break from all of life's responsibilities without running from our problems."

Even as I said that last bit and even imagined the two of us living off grid without worrying about the issues within the supernatural world, I knew that neither of us would ever be able to walk away from things we'd been fighting for. It was nice to picture, though.

"I love you," he murmured against my cheek.

"I love you, too."

Maciah turned for the shower, and I moved back to the bed, reaching for my phone. We were going to need each other more than ever, and I'd do whatever it took to ease the guilt Maciah was clinging to.

CHAPTER 3

As soon as night fell, we left the hotel and headed back to the nest. The drive was tense, and the devastation that filled me when we pulled into the driveway took my breath away.

I'd been getting better at tucking the sorrow away, but seeing the house completely destroyed undid every bit of progress I'd made in the hotel room.

Charred remains were piled where the once ten-thousand-square-foot structure used to be. The roof had caved in. The walls were gone from most of the front and right side of the house. Yet, I could still see the framework for the staircase within the center of it all.

Maciah's emotions were varying between rage and mourning. After he'd opened up to me earlier, I better understood him. On top of how much he cared but rarely showed, he'd also worked hard to build the life he had created within the nest...and in hours, it had been turned into ash. It wasn't right or fair.

We stepped out of the SUV and walked toward the house. Drips of water sounded from inside, and the stench of smoke made me gag.

"Do you think there is anything to salvage?" I asked, trying to hold on to the slightest sliver of hope that coming back here wasn't just going to torture us more.

He shrugged. "Possibly, but there is so much rubble, it would take days to dig through everything carefully enough to find anything worth taking."

As we stepped closer to the warmth of the buried embers, I focused on the sound of water from the firefighters. I didn't know how long they'd been gone, but the plinking noise echoed around us in the quiet of the night.

I reached out to the rose bushes when I got near where the front entrance used to be. The leaves and petals were covered in ash. When I swiped my fingers over them, the charcoal residue burned my skin.

I jerked my hand back and hissed, leaning in closer. "This wasn't an ordinary fire, Maciah. Not even by magical standards."

His mouth downturned. "I didn't think it was. I'd known it was bad when I mentioned the dark magic earlier, but if the ash is burning you, then it's worse than I thought."

I read between the lines. Maciah had been holding on to a small hope that some of the vampires had survived, but if the ash had burned me like metal, the chances of finding any survivors lessened significantly.

Hope was a beast, one that was now ripping the cracks in my heart wide open as I stared helplessly at the remains of the nest.

Maciah's fury rose, and he began ripping charred pieces of the house away from where he wanted to be. I wasn't sure what he was doing, but I wasn't going to stop him. He needed this. He needed to tear his home apart and get the rage out in some way.

At least this way was cathartic.

I followed after him, doing my best to avoid the ash while searching the ground for anything worth checking out. There wasn't much to see other than waterlogged flooring and crispy bits of furniture or structural pieces that had fallen from the upper level.

As we neared the back of the house, there was still a section of the second floor that could be accessed if someone had a ladder or the capability of jumping more than a dozen feet in the air.

"Be careful." I barely got the words out before Maciah was leaping into the air showing that vampires were capable of just that.

He landed with a soft thud. The floor groaned beneath his weight, and he turned back to me. "Stay down there. I won't be long."

Yeah, I had no problem listening to that. I continued to push through the debris, doing my best to ignore the fact that I was ruining the new clothes Maciah had bought me, and I didn't have anything else as back-up.

As I got to the rear hallway, I tried to enter a room that was sealed off, but the wood had swelled from the water and didn't want to budge. I was one second away from kicking it in when the faintest noise caught my attention.

It was so soft, I thought I was imagining things, but as I stilled and focused, there was no denying the sounds of someone screaming.

I tried not to let hope blossom inside me again. I couldn't handle being wrong, but there was no stopping the relief as I heard the voice a third time.

"Maciah!" I called out and turned around to head further into the house, tearing through whatever was in my way, ignoring the burns on my palms as I did so.

Maciah was right behind me when I made it to the basement stairs that led to the gym. There were steel posts jammed in front of the door, blocking the way down.

"Do you hear them?" I asked while trying to figure out how we were going to get in there.

"I hear something." He nudged me aside and took off his suit jacket that I could see already had a couple of tears in it. Then he wrapped the material around the beams.

I stepped out of the way as he manhandled the steel, ripping the posts away and flinging them further down the hall. His palms were red and blistered, even with the jacket keeping a barrier between his skin and the metal, but he didn't show any sign of pain.

Once the doorway was free, he kicked it in, only to find the stairwell full of more wreckage.

"We're down here!" The voice became clearer, but it was weak and muffled, so I couldn't identify who it might belong to.

"Hurry," I said to Maciah as we worked together to haul the burned materials out of our way.

What felt like hours later, and lots of injuries from the ash and metal we had to dig through, we finally got to the bottom and entered the gym. The air was smoky, and there were no lights, but we could see a group of people huddled in the corner. Four of them were lying on the floor, one was standing closer to us, and another was hunched over on their knees near the prone vampires.

Zeke's face came into view first as he stepped closer. Burn marks covered his exposed skin, and his eyes were a dark crimson.

Without thinking, I ran to him and gently wrapped my arms around his waist. Tears pricked the back of my eyes as his hands came around my back.

He winced from the movement, and I pulled back. "Are you okay?"

Zeke nodded and pointed to his throat.

"Can you talk?" I asked.

He shook his head and grimaced.

"We're going to get you all out of here," Maciah said as he moved past us.

I followed him. Nikki was the one hunched over her knees. I went to her, gently lifting her chin. "Can you talk?"

"Enough. I was the one screaming when I heard you guys." Her voice was hoarse. Whatever air they'd been breathing had done a number on them.

I glanced around, trying not to panic. "Did Rachel…"

Nikki gestured with her head toward the bodies on the floor. "She's on the right. She hasn't been awake for the last couple of hours, but she also hasn't turned to ash, so there's hope."

Next to Rachel's body were three piles of ash. Nine vampires had made it to the basement, but not all of them survived. I shook my head, trying not to lose my composure, so we could focus on helping those who had made it.

I turned to Maciah. "We need blood."

"I have more in the back of the SUV. I got enough earlier to last us for a week since we weren't sure what we were doing yet."

My hand covered Nikki's. "I'm going to be right back."

She coughed and groaned in pain, but I didn't stick around to console her. The quicker we got them blood, the quicker we could get them out of the basement. They needed nourishment to speed up the healing process and help remove whatever metal they'd ingested.

Swirls of fury and glee filled my chest. I couldn't believe they were alive, but what they'd been through…

only a sick, twisted person could have thought of such a wicked plan.

Silas was smart, but I was beginning to think he had nothing to do with what happened here.

I arrived at the SUV and opened the trunk, grabbing the cooler then racing back within mere seconds. My chest was already feeling the effects of being in the house, and I'd only been there maybe fifteen minutes. The thought of how much pain the others were in from having been there hours was almost too much to fathom.

When I arrived back at the gym, there were no longer four vampires on the ground. There were only three and another new pile of ash.

"Damn it." I rushed forward, hating how much I prayed the missing one wasn't Rachel. It was a selfish thought, but one I couldn't prevent from circling my mind.

A small sigh of relief left me when I saw Zeke kneeling over her, trying to coax her awake. I opened the cooler of blood, handed out bags to each of the coherent vampires, and grabbed three more for the ones still not awake.

Zeke tore the corner off the first bag, and instead of taking care of himself first, he gently opened Rachel's mouth, feeding her before he worried about himself.

Maciah took a bag from the cooler as I gave one to Nikki before going to help those still on the ground. Maciah was already working on the second, so I moved to the third. With all of the ash covering his face, I wasn't sure who he was, but that didn't mean anything. Every one of them was worth saving.

I dribbled a quarter of the bag into his mouth and Nikki joined me, her eyes brighter. "Let me help," she said, finally able to talk normally.

I handed her the bag in my hand while I reached for more from the cooler. By the time I had it open, the vampire we were working on began to cough. I helped Nikki roll him onto his side as droplets of blood spilled from his lips. My hand rubbed over his back, on fire from the metal flecks in the ash, but that was the least of my worries.

"You're going to be okay," I said softly, holding the bag in front of his face.

Nikki leaned in closer and murmured, "Gabe."

I nodded, silently thanking her for the name as Gabe's hands shakily moved for the bag. I lifted him up so that his head was propped against my stomach and his back rested on my knees.

"Easy, Gabe," I said when he began to drink too quickly.

His gulps slowed, and he let out a small sigh. "I thought I was dead."

"You're not that lucky," I joked, probably too soon, but I couldn't help myself. The stress rolling through me was too much to handle without a bit of sarcasm.

Nikki let out a sigh of relief before moving on to help with the others still not awake yet as I stayed with Gabe.

He finished the bag, then sat up on his own. I turned

to check on the others to find Maciah's vampire was also coherent, but Zeke was still kneeling over an unconscious Rachel.

Nikki was sitting next to Zeke, holding Rachel's hand. "Come on, Rach. You're not allowed to give up now," she pleaded.

Any hope that I'd been building was dwindling quickly as I took in Rachel's ashen face. Maciah bent to her other side, and I sat at her feet.

There was nothing any of us could do as Zeke slowly continued to feed her blood. My hands gently held her legs, and I silently begged my best friend to wake up.

CHAPTER 4

MINUTES OF TENSE SILENCE PASSED. THE SECOND BLOOD BAG was almost empty, but there were no changes in Rachel. The other two vampires stood around us, waiting quietly as well.

"Should we move her?" Nikki suggested.

"Getting her outside might not be a bad idea. The air in here is still burning my lungs," Zeke said.

I agreed with him. The effects of the magically enhanced fire were still heavy in the air, even if there were no flames flickering.

"We need to do so carefully. There's no telling what kind of internal injuries she might have that are preventing her from waking," Maciah said as he got a better hold on Rachel's head.

I gently held her feet and legs as Zeke and Nikki both placed their hands under her back and thighs. I hoped the movements would cause Rachel to groan or give any sign of discomfort. Even pain was better than the nothingness we were getting from her, but my hope didn't make a bit of difference. There were no changes to her slack facial expression and limp extremities.

Gabe and the other vampire I could now tell was Jazz by the red-orange hair peeking through the ash covering him went ahead of us, making sure the path was still clear to get outside.

As we moved through the house, I could see headlights pulling into the driveway. Nick and Eddie were back from the hospital, hopefully with good news about Dave.

We set Rachel onto the grass a good twenty feet from the house. I inhaled deeply, ignoring the burning in my throat as I double-checked that the air around us was clean enough for Rachel.

Zeke took Maciah's spot as he went to greet Eddie and Nick. I slid into Zeke's spot, holding Rachel's hand and watching her face for any sign of movement.

"I'm going to grab more blood," Nikki said.

I looked up at Zeke. There were matching trails down both of his cheeks where his tears had cleared away the ash from his dark skin. My heart hurt for him. He and Rachel had just realized there could be something more between them, and they might not ever get the chance to see where things could end up.

Nikki came back with another blood bag, giving it to Zeke so he could continue to be the one to feed Rachel.

I locked eyes with Nikki, and the concern rolling off

her matched my own. There was nothing we could do other than pray our friend woke up soon.

Maciah stood behind me, his hands on my shoulders as we all waited, hoping like hell that the nest wasn't going to lose any more of its members.

Zeke finished giving Rachel the third bag and bent down to whisper in her ear. "Come on, baby. Open those gorgeous eyes."

My throat burned from the effort it took to keep my own tears at bay. As grateful as I was that we'd found at least some of the vampires still alive, I knew losing Rachel after thinking she was still alive would overshadow any positive emotions we'd allowed in.

I squeezed her hand tight. "Come on, Rach. We need your sunshine to keep us going."

There was a twitch in her fingers, and I tensed.

"What is it?" Maciah asked.

I didn't answer as I waited for it to happen again. My eyes went to Nikki's, wondering if she'd felt anything, but she didn't look up.

Then, it happened again.

"She's moving," I said in awe.

Zeke began to frantically stroke Rachel's cheeks, brushing the long strands of her hair back. "That's right. I knew you wouldn't give up easily."

"If you wake up, I promise to give you the girliest girl's night ever," Nikki added.

Finally, Rachel sucked in a breath then began choking until Zeke pulled her up.

Fresh tears fell down my face, this time from happiness instead of grief. I backed up, giving her some space, and allowed Maciah to pull me into his waiting arms.

We might have gone from a nest of over forty vampires to only nine, but that was more than we believed we had as of this morning, and it was worth being thankful for.

"Whoever did this, deserves..." Rachel's words were cut off by another coughing fit, but Nikki gladly finished her sentence.

"To be tarred and feathered, then burned alive? To have their skin peeled slowly from their body while they're awake? To be stabbed with thousands of needles that slowly burn them to death?"

"All of the above," I said before she continued to go too far down the rabbit hole of murderous ideas.

I bent back down to Rachel's side, my voice rough with emotion. "I didn't think I'd ever see you again."

"You guys wouldn't survive a day without me," she said with a small smile.

"You're absolutely right." I got up and pulled Maciah away from Zeke and Rachel. Nikki and the others got the hint as well. The two of them deserved a few moments to themselves after almost dying.

"How are things at the hospital?" Maciah asked Eddie.

"Good. We stayed until Dave was awake. He said to

call him when you two weren't busy. He might have more information that could help us," Eddie answered.

I took a deep breath, even more grateful that Dave and the few vampires around us were all okay.

"I don't think Silas did this," Maciah said, nodding at the house.

I scoffed. "I was thinking the same thing earlier. He's resourceful, but whatever this was took wit I'm not sure he contained."

"What happened?" Nick asked.

Gabe and Jazz stepped forward, but Nikki beat them to answering. "When the bombs started dropping, we tried to get out the front, but the flames were blocking the exits every way we ran. Zeke got the idea to head downstairs. We grabbed as many vampires as we could, but not enough." She wiped a stray tear from her cheek before proceeding.

"The walls were caving in around us. The air was burning our lungs. We raced to the gym and moved to the furthest corner away from the door. We heard the entrance closing in, but figured we were better off being trapped than trying to get through the flames again."

"How come you didn't dig your way out when the fire was put out?" Maciah asked.

"We tried, but the metal we'd inhaled weakened all of us. Zeke knew you'd come back for us, so we just focused on staying alive instead," she answered, then glanced at the house. "I can't believe this happened."

"What are we going to do now?" Gabe asked.

"Amersyn suggested that we head to LA, and I agree with her. We have food and some supplies there that will hold us over until we can re-evaluate things," Maciah answered.

"We can also ask the other supernaturals for help," I said. Asking for assistance might not have been Maciah's thing in the past, nor was it mine, but I wasn't too proud to see that we couldn't do this alone. Not now.

Maciah nodded but didn't say anything else.

Zeke and Rachel joined us. He was holding her up, and she was wincing through the pain still coursing inside her body, but there was a light in her eyes that said she wasn't giving up.

"To the airport? Or do we have anything else to do here in Portland?" Eddie asked.

Maciah glanced around what was left of his home and glowered. "To the airport."

I reached for his hand, sending thoughts of comfort toward him. We had lost so much, but finding these five vampires still alive was a huge win, considering the circumstances. If we didn't focus on that, then we'd drown in the negatives, which wouldn't help us win against whoever had done this.

The more time that passed, the more I was beginning to believe Viktor had been pulling the strings for much longer than any of us realized.

Not only had we known Silas was likely working with him, but Dmitri had admitted to me that he was attempting to double-cross Viktor. We also knew that

Viktor's men were the ones to recruit Simon from Crossroads.

My biggest problem with knowing all of that was realizing that I didn't know enough about Viktor, and it was time that changed.

CHAPTER 5

All of the vampires seemed to need time to themselves once we were on the plane. With Maciah flying, I had a minute to myself as well, which I thought would be a good thing. I was wrong. I only ended up spiraling, something I'd thought I was done with.

My erratic emotions had nothing to do with being a newborn or needing to eat and everything to do with some craptastic PTSD. Memories of being homeless and alone hit me hard as I thought of everything I'd lost in the last two days. Not only the vampires who had died, but of once again having to start over.

It was as if I was doomed to never have a sense of permanency. Normally, I wasn't much of a dweller on the horridness of my past, but with fresh wounds, I couldn't help myself. After losing my family, I went straight into the arms of someone who turned out to be an insecure and controlling man.

After that, I bounced around until finding a place in Pete's gym. Then, that was burned down. My condo was destroyed, and now so was Maciah's nest. The one place that brought me a sense of peace once I'd finally accepted Maciah and the others into my life.

But as I looked at Rachel sleeping on the other side of the plane, Zeke keeping watch over her, and Nikki staring out the window with pondering eyes, I forced the negative thoughts out of my head and headed toward the front of the plane.

I passed Eddie, Nick, Gabe, and Jazz, all sitting together and playing a card game while smiling. I knew that if they could stay strong, then so could I.

I continued until I found Maciah in the cockpit. When I opened the door, his eyes met mine and he reached for me.

"You're hurting," he said, reading my emotions.

"We all are," I replied.

"But yours is heavy. Just because we all lost something last night doesn't mean that you can't express how painful this all is for you. You made me do so earlier and, as much as talking about the past made me uncomfortable, I won't deny it helped. You should do the same."

I knew that, and it was exactly why I also knew that I couldn't ever give up what I'd found since Maciah inserted himself into my life as my protector.

So, instead of continuing to keep everything to myself,

I took a seat next to Maciah and accepted his offer of a listening ear.

My eyes burned from crying more than I wanted throughout the day, but I finally felt like I could breathe easier after talking to Maciah. He'd let me ramble and held my hand until we made it to Los Angeles.

We landed with only a few small bumps on the runway, and then the nine of us disembarked the plane. Seeing all of us together reminded me that I needed to be at my best, and the strongest version of myself didn't dwell on the things she couldn't change. She only focused on what needed to be done in order to keep putting one foot in front of the other.

Maciah and Zeke went to find us transportation to the house since we hadn't had time to arrange it before our departure. I stayed put with Rachel and Nikki, hugging them again now that they were both awake and healed.

I wasn't normally one for physical affection, but after believing they were dead for hours on end, having them close felt right.

"I should have almost died a long time ago," Rachel said as I released her.

I punched her in the arm. "That isn't funny. No more hugs for you."

She nudged me with her hip. "I'm sorry, Am. That

was a poorly given joke. I have no intentions of going through something like today again."

"Too soon for jokes," I grumbled even though I appreciated her attempts to make me laugh.

"How about we stop talking about almost dying and more about the fact Rachel and Zeke were openly pawing at each other on the plane before we landed?" Nikki suggested, and that was something I could get behind since I'd missed it while talking with Maciah.

Rachel grinned and bit her lip in feigned embarrassment.

"Does that mean the two of you are done taking things slow?" I asked.

She shrugged. "We didn't really talk about it, but it feels that way."

"Sometimes actions are more appropriate than words when you already know how the other person feels," Nikki said, and I completely agreed.

Nikki looked up toward the stars, and I knew she was missing the love she once had. Likely both the one she had with her husband and then again with Bennett.

"Should we do something for the vampires that didn't make it?" I asked. As grateful as I was to have my friends back, the ones who died in the fight against Silas and the explosion deserved a proper send-off if vampires did such a thing.

"We've never had losses this big. Normally, we throw a party, but I don't know if that would be wise right now," Rachel said.

I thought about that as two sets of headlights came around the corner and into the parking lot. Maciah and Zeke were each driving blacked-out Range Rovers and waved for us to all get in.

Gabe and Jazz headed for Zeke's SUV, getting into the back and leaving the front seat likely for Rachel. She didn't hesitate to head that way, either.

Nick and Eddie joined me and Nikki in the vehicle with Maciah.

As I buckled up, Maciah reached over to brush his fingers over my thigh. "Everything good?"

"Yep," I answered, and for the first time all day, I meant it.

He nodded and sped off toward the airport exit with Zeke driving right behind us.

The ride to the house was quiet as everyone watched out the window for anything that didn't belong. We didn't know what other tricks Viktor might have had ready for us, and we couldn't be too careful, especially as we got closer to the house.

Maciah slowly pulled into the driveway, rolling down his window and looking up into the sky. I did the same as soon as I caught on to what he was worried about.

"I don't hear any drones," I said a few minutes later, and we were only halfway up the driveway.

"Neither do I, but we all need to be on guard," Maciah said as he continued to pull up to the house.

Everything looked just as it did the last time I was

there. The air was warm compared to Portland, and I couldn't scent anything that didn't belong.

Everyone was out of the vehicles now, but nobody headed inside. Having your house blown up was hard to recover from.

Deciding they all needed a bit of encouragement, I took the first step onto the walkway leading toward the front door. Maciah was at my side in the next second, and we went up the few steps together.

"We won't live in fear," I said softly as my fingers curled around the handle.

He nodded, and I pushed open the door. The hum of the refrigerator was the only thing I could hear as we let the door swing fully open.

Rachel, Zeke, and Nikki were right behind us, and I caught sight of Eddie and Nick heading around the back. Paranoid? Probably. Smart? Absolutely.

The rest of us entered the house, and a collective feeling of relief swept over me when nothing out of the ordinary happened.

My phone vibrated in my back pocket, scaring the hell out of me. I flinched before reaching to answer the call, glad to see My Bartender as the name calling.

"Hey, Dave," I said as I put the phone on speaker.

"Hey, Dave? That's all you have to say after I almost died for you?" he snapped.

I held the phone further away from me, confusion rolling through me. Dave had never been angry with me.

"I'm kidding, Amersyn," he added when I didn't reply.

Freaking people needed to realize it was too soon for jokes. Regardless of the fact that I'd been the first to make one. Lesson learned.

"Right. How are you doing?" I asked as I headed toward the couch. Only Maciah followed me.

He groaned and I could hear the crinkle of a hospital pillow followed by Steve's voice. "I said you're not allowed to move."

Dave sighed. "I've been better. How about you? Eddie and Nick wouldn't say what happened, but I know something did."

"Silas or Viktor blew up our house. Only a handful of vampires made it out alive," I said solemnly.

"Damn, Am. I'm sorry, and I'm even more sorry for having to jump straight into business, but I've been trying to reach you for a while."

I grimaced. "Yeah, sorry about that. Some things came up."

"I heard. You're not who either of us thought, but I hope you know that's not a bad thing." I could hear the smile in his voice, which made one appear on my own face.

"No, it's definitely not as bad as I would have once thought. So, what did you need to share? Steve mentioned stuff about Simon already."

"Simon wants to become a vampire. The last time he was in the bar, I heard him begging a few of the bloodsuckers he was with when I crept around the corner pretending to dust."

I snorted. "Dusting? In that bar?"

"I know, but it worked. Anyway, the vampires told him he had to earn that privilege. He promised to do whatever they wanted, and that's when the plan to kill you was first mentioned around me," Dave said.

"Those are the same vampires working for Viktor that you mentioned before, right?" I asked.

"That's the thing. I'm not sure. They kept a rotation after a while. The same group of three or four never repeated after the first few days they were looking for you. But they all did the same thing. Sat in the same corner booth, ordering only one drink each, and would sit there for hours until just before closing."

"Why would they do that day after day?" I asked, not really expecting an answer.

"They were making a statement," Maciah said.

"That's what I was beginning to think as well. The usual hunters stopped coming into the bar after the first week. Even other supernaturals got leery of hanging out. The atmosphere became tense instead of the usual loud and obnoxious vibe I've always known," Dave said.

"So, what does that mean for us?" I asked.

"It means they wanted people to know they were there, and they were looking for a hunter," Maciah answered.

I had wondered why the hunter app was so quiet, and

maybe this was why. Everyone was freaked out about those new vampires continually hanging around.

"Why did any of that make you so worried about me?" I asked Dave, because it really wasn't anything too out of the ordinary. People wanted to kill me all the time before I even met Maciah.

"Because of what I heard Simon agree to. After that conversation with the vampires, they stopped coming in and the hunters returned, but they weren't the same ones I was used to. They all followed Simon's lead and I was once again questioned about you. My attitude might have been what got me taken."

Dave had shown he cared, and if the bartender cared about a hunter, then to anyone else, that likely meant the hunter cared about the bartender. I understood better why they'd used Dave as leverage, even though I'd been careful not to give him too much public attention.

"What did Simon agree to?" I asked.

"He said he would lure you out and create a trap for Viktor's vampires to take you, but something happened. I don't know what changed," Dave said.

"Silas happened. He reached out to Viktor," I said as the pieces of this tangled web began to come together.

"Who's Silas?" Dave asked.

"The man who took you," I answered.

"No, Simon took me, and the same vampires I saw in the bar beat the hell out of me," Dave replied, seeming very sure of that.

Maciah looked at me, his eyes darkening. "Silas was

working for Viktor the whole time and we had no clue. You were right. Viktor sent the drones. He's been calling the shots ever since he realized you were alive. Only he didn't expect me to find you in that alley when I did."

I remembered the night I first saw Maciah clearly, and wondered how weird it was that the group of vampires who attacked me would have been seeking vengeance for a vampire they could easily replace. Maybe Maciah was right. Maybe those vampires hadn't just been out to avenge their friend. Maybe Viktor had convinced that particular group of bloodsuckers to be the first test against me.

Putting what I'd already thought, what Dave added, and what Maciah said together, I could see the big picture more clearly, and I decided there was no question about any of it. Viktor had known what he was doing the whole time.

"Why didn't he just kill me himself?" I asked.

"Because vampires get bored. He's having fun playing with you," Maciah grumbled.

"I agree with whoever that is," Dave said, and I smirked.

"That's Maciah."

"Is that the one Steve said you were draped all over as you left the hospital?"

I groaned. "I don't 'drape' over anyone."

Dave laughed, then groaned from the action. "I'm happy for you, Am. Just stay alive long enough to enjoy what you've found."

"Thank you, Dave."

"I'm due for my sponge bath with Nurse Steve, so I'm going to go, but check in with me soon," he said.

"You're welcome to come out here where we can protect you if you don't mind hanging with a bunch of vampires," I said, half joking.

"I think I've had enough of vampires to last me a lifetime, but the offer is appreciated. We'll be okay here given I don't plan to head back to Crossroads anytime soon. Just worry about you and stay safe, Amersyn."

"Thanks, Dave."

He hung up, and I met Maciah's gaze. "Viktor needs to die."

"And soon," he agreed.

CHAPTER 6

After Maciah and I got off the phone with Dave, we decided that everyone had been through a hellish day, and it was time to unwind. All of us went our separate ways, and I smiled at the fact that Zeke and Rachel headed toward the same bedroom.

Knowing that they and Nikki were alive went a long way to prevent me from worrying about anything else at the moment.

I went to the bathroom and turned on the shower, groaning that I was once again without clean clothes.

"I'll throw everything in the washer. You can wear one of my shirts in the meantime if you want, until everything is cleaned," Maciah said as he moved in behind me, helping to undress me.

His fingers left a trail of fire up my sides as he pulled my charred shirt over my head while I unbuttoned my pants, kicking out of them in seconds, cringing as spots of ash hit new parts of my skin.

He brushed my hair to the side, pressed his lips to my shoulder, and unclipped my bra. The straps fell down my arms, and Maciah slowly slid them off me before whispering in my ear, "I'll be right back to join you."

I nodded and watched as he grabbed a towel before leaving the bathroom, shutting the door behind him.

My hands held on to the edge of the counter as I let my head drop down. A curtain of hair fell around me, and I took a deep breath. Only one more vampire to kill before things could settle in to a new normal.

If I was wrong and there were more psychos out there that wanted me dead for whatever reason, I was going to lose it, but for the time being, I was counting on Viktor being the last pain in my side. At least for the foreseeable future.

I lifted my head back up, staring at myself in the mirror. Everything about me had changed, but I wasn't as disappointed by that fact as I thought I would be.

I might not be who I thought, but that didn't matter anymore. There were no more reservations about being a vampire left inside me. No doubts that my family would be proud of me. No ill feelings toward who my father really was and how my mother had kept that information from me.

Even as everything around us seemed to be falling apart, I knew I was only getting stronger. There would never be a time when I gave up. No matter how much I wanted to, or how awful things became, Viktor was going to learn that he'd picked the wrong vampire heir to come after.

I wasn't weak. I was a fighter, and I'd keep fighting for the family I lost and for the one I'd gained along the way.

My eyes had officially settled into the dark maroon color that humans would assume to be more mahogany than anything else, but with my vampire eyes, I could see past the surface and into the deeper layers that made the color more stunning than human eyes could see.

I ran my hand over my tattoo, remembering why I'd gotten the marks in the first place, and I was eager for my vengeance to be done with.

I didn't regret the path I'd set out on, but after spending the last seven years killing vampires, I was ready to live life more for myself than out of guilt for surviving when my family hadn't.

The mirror began to fog up, allowing me to shake off the reminders of my past as I turned for the shower. As soon as I tilted my head back and the hot water cascaded against my sensitive skin, I was sighing in relief.

Closing my eyes, I let the steady stream cover my face and soak my hair while rubbing my hands over my eyes.

A cool burst of air blew around me, but the coldness was quickly replaced by Maciah's warm hands. "There is nothing more beautiful than seeing you with your guard down."

My lips lifted into a small smile as I brought my head forward and opened my eyes. My hands wrapped around

Maciah's neck, tugging him closer to me. "I can only do so because you helped me see it was okay to trust people again."

He leaned in and kissed me briefly, then reached for the soap beside us. Lathering up his hands, he moved them first over my shoulders and neck, then worked his way down my body. The more he touched me, the further undone I became.

By the time he finished, I was barely breathing and in desperate need of more from him. Except he had charcoal smeared on his arms and deserved the same treatment. So, I repaid the favor, moving Maciah until we'd switched places and he was standing under the showerhead.

The vanilla smell from the body wash had nothing on the natural scent Maciah exuded, but it reminded me that too much time had passed since I had taken a moment to enjoy the small things, like how much just the sweet aroma of Maciah attracted me to him.

As I scrubbed at the char from the fire on Maciah's skin, his hands massaged the conditioner into my hair. Once his arms were clean, I worked my way over his stomach, caressing every dip and curve of the muscles that rippled beneath my touch.

My hands cupped his balls, and I grinned up at him. "Can't forget these."

His eyes darkened to nearly black in return. "I'd expect nothing less from you."

As his hard length grew under my touch, Maciah

spun me around so that my back was to him and I was standing under the water with him.

His dick twitched against my ass as he rinsed the conditioner from my long strands. As soon as he was done, I turned the water off and reached for a towel to at least dry my hair a little before we finished what we—or maybe just I—had started.

I bent forward to wring the water out, but I barely even had the towel around the long strands before Maciah had me cradled in his arms and was taking me into the bedroom.

"I'm all wet," I said, pointing out the obvious.

He smirked. "Just the way I like you."

Well, that wasn't what I'd meant, but he also wasn't wrong.

Maciah tossed me onto the bed, and I spread my soaking hair out behind me as he grabbed my ankles, pulling me closer to the edge of the mattress.

He brought my feet up as he stood in front of the bed, kissing each of the arches before sliding his hands slowly down each leg and wrapping them around his waist.

His fingers barely touched my center when my hips bucked, silently begging for him to keep the teasing to a minimum. He smirked and leaned forward to kiss my stomach, causing my back to arch while my chest rose and fell rapidly as the anticipation built between us.

I reached my hands toward his shoulders, hoping to pull him on top of me, but he moved out of the way before I could get a good hold.

"Too many hours have passed since I've been able to properly love you. I won't be rushed, but I promise, you'll thank me later."

"How about you rush through this first round and torture me the second go around? I have no doubt I'd thank you for that as well," I countered, trying to use my ankles to bring him closer and failing.

He shook his head at me as he broke out of the hold I had around his hips, then lowered to his knees. Before I could protest, his mouth covered my center and his tongue flicked over my clit, making me cry out from the instant relief his touch offered.

My skin tingled and heated as he sucked harder on my core, adding his fingers into the mix.

The orgasm growing inside me built up quicker and faster than I was used to, making me tighten around his fingers until I wondered if this wasn't punishment for my lack of patience.

Except punishment didn't usually come with moans of pleasure, so I pushed those thoughts aside as I lifted my hips in time with his movements. My fingers tangled into his long strands as I held him right where I wanted when I got close to coming, but Maciah seemed to have other plans.

Just as I was about to crest over a glorious sex-induced hill, Maciah pulled his hand and face back, then cupped my center with his palm. "Not yet."

My lip lifted into a snarl as I thought to yell at him. Though, the chance to do so was gone in an instant. He flipped me over and plunged inside me from behind, pressing my back down so that my ass went higher into the air, then he stilled as I wiggled against him.

Torturously slow, he pulled out and slammed back into me. My fingers curled around the comforter as I let my head fall until my forehead rested against the bed.

He reached around and pressed his fingers over my clit, then moved at a steadier pace. By then, I was nearly panting, needily pressing back against him while matching his every thrust, wanting every inch of him that I could get inside me.

Maciah slid his other hand over my spine before gripping my hip and picking up speed. Just as I began to tighten around him, he pulled out of me again and flipped me onto my back.

I leaned up with my hand raised, ready to smack some sense into him, but he was on top of me, kissing my intentions away as if he'd known exactly what to expect.

As I opened my mouth to him, he spread my legs open, and I sighed as he fit perfectly inside me with one fluid thrust, almost as if we were made for each other.

He tried to keep me distracted as his tongue danced with mine, but I wasn't falling for his antics a third time. I brought my hands forward, gripping his hips and rocking against him, taking what I needed from him.

Maciah's breath moved over my cheek and down my neck until he was sucking on the spot behind my ear. My fangs elongated, and the sudden urge to bite him came over me.

I dug my nails into his shoulder, unsure if that was an instinct I wanted to act on. Then, he nipped at my neck, scraping his own fangs over my skin.

I shoved any hesitation aside as I let my sharp teeth sink into the top of his shoulder and let out a stifled cry as he did the same to me.

Once again, emotions exploded inside me, moving between us, drawing the bond we shared to the surface and solidifying the love I knew we both had for each other.

His blood was unlike any I'd drank, and I craved for more as I eagerly took from him, but as his movements above me continued to increase in speed, I was fighting a battle between my natural cravings and the sexual wants only Maciah could draw from me.

My fangs began to retract on their own after another moment, and I flicked my tongue over the puncture marks I'd made, watching as they faded into two pink circles before my eyes.

Maciah's tongue did the same but continued a path back up to my ear before he nipped at my lobe.

As my moans got louder, I tried to quiet them, worried he was going to try to withdraw from me again, but then he moved so that we were staring into each other's eyes. One of his hands held him up and the other lifted my ass up, so he could burrow deeper inside me.

With our gazes locked, any concerns I'd previously had fell away. I focused only on Maciah and the shared love between us, memorizing every sharp line of his face and the way his dark hair fell around his eyes as they watched me.

My core tightened around him as his grip did the same to my hips. Our speed picked up, and I was suddenly thankful he'd made me wait for this moment to come with him. Just like he knew I would be. Cocky vampire.

Our bond swirled between us, and my fingers wrapped tightly around his biceps as my vision faltered. I threw my head back, succumbing to the euphoria ravaging my insides, and cried out as Maciah's sweaty body settled on top of mine.

Once I found the strength to open my eyes, I tried and failed to find words.

"You're…" I wasn't sure what to call him. Evil? Genius? Delectable? All of the above.

He grinned, lifting himself up so he was resting on his elbows. "As long as I'm yours, nothing else matters."

And that was the truth.

No matter what we faced, I knew with Maciah at my side, we would survive.

CHAPTER 7

WE WAITED UNTIL JUST BEFORE DAWN TO CRAWL OUT OF BED, and muscles I didn't even know *could* be sore were sore. Though, I had no complaints about that. I'd needed the connection with Maciah, and he seemed to have needed it as well.

Maciah went downstairs first and pulled our clothes from the dryer they'd been switched to a couple hours prior. When he returned, he frowned, setting the clothes on the bed.

"What's wrong?" I asked, grabbing my underwear and bra first.

"There are a lot of windows in this house."

The sun was a big setback for me and a weakness for our group. If Viktor attacked when I was limited as to where I could go, then we didn't stand a chance.

"Is there any way around the sensitivity?" I asked, knowing there were some vampire secrets not widely shared. Maybe there was one I hadn't thought to ask about yet.

"Possibly, but we'd need a witch. We can head to Warlock tonight and see if we can find one, along with information about Viktor," Maciah said as he began getting dressed in clothes he had stashed here already.

Going out and doing something was good, not only for our group, but also for Viktor to know he hadn't crushed us by destroying the nest.

"Rachel mentioned that a party was usually thrown in honor of vampires who died. Should we do something here? I know it won't be the same, but they deserve to be honored," I said, unable to let go of the ones who died, even if I hadn't been close to them.

"I'll think of something. Zeke might have already done so as well, so I'll check with him," Maciah answered while buttoning up his shirt.

"No suit coat for you?" I asked when I didn't see it with the rest of our things.

He shook his head. "Maybe later. Too much work to do today around the house so we can make it safe for you to leave the room. We only have blackout blinds in the bedrooms."

"What about clothes for the others? Do they have what they need? Or do we need to go shopping for more than one outfit for the rest of us?" I asked.

"I have a laptop in the closet. I figured you could order some stuff to be delivered here. I'll have the guys get a list of what they need together as well. I'm sure Rachel and Nikki have plenty in their rooms."

Online shopping would be a good way to pass the day since there wasn't much we could do about Viktor until the sun went down.

I finished getting dressed, grabbed the laptop from the shelf in the closet, and went back to give Maciah a kiss. "I'm going to find Rachel and Nikki."

He grimaced. "I need to cover all of the windows before you leave the room. The sun will be shining anytime now. How about I get them and you ladies spend the morning in here while I finish blocking out the sun?"

"Thank you," I said to Maciah before kissing him again. I didn't want to feel the way I had in the car when I'd been exposed to the sun the day before. My skin itched just at the reminder.

He blurred out of the bedroom, and I made the bed before Rachel and Nikki arrived. They came into the room with steaming travel mugs of blood-flavored coffee. Seriously, I had the best friends ever.

Rachel handed me one of the cups. "Miss us?"

"Only a little," I said as I snatched the goodness from her hand and took a long pull of the sweet liquid.

They sat on the bed, and I grabbed the laptop from the nightstand before joining them.

"Maciah said we were going to do a little online shopping," Nikki said, not seeming super excited.

"I need clothes. I'm sure you guys have stuff here, but

it would be nice to have my own things to wear," I said, opening the internet browser.

Rachel clapped her hands. "I know several stores around here who will deliver as long as you spend enough."

Normally I wasn't much of a spender on clothes, but after the hell we went through, I had no problem meeting whatever minimums there were to get delivery.

"Did Maciah give you his credit card?" Rachel asked.

I laughed so hard the whole bed shook. "Yeah, no. I don't need Maciah's money. I have my own." I even had my card number memorized for emergencies just like this. I'd flag it lost as soon as we were done, then have a new one expedited.

I nodded at Nikki before I started looking things up. "Do you want to talk about anything?"

We were a lot alike, and I wasn't going to push her, but I could sense the unease she was feeling like it was my own. Her melancholy pressed lightly down on my chest, leaving a reminder that nothing was how it should be any longer.

"Not really." She forced a smile and moved closer to me. "Let me pull up the places Rachel was talking about."

She took the laptop from me. I'd gladly let her do whatever she wanted as long as it helped ease what was going on inside that head of hers.

Already knowing Nikki was out of sorts, I didn't ask Rachel about Zeke. Instead, I brought up the call from Dave.

"How is he doing?" Rachel asked.

"He sounded good, and I think they're letting him out of the hospital soon. I invited him and Steve to come stay with us."

Nikki raised a brow. "Two humans staying in a house with nine vampires? That could make things more interesting."

"Hopefully not. Though, we probably won't find out. He didn't seem keen on the idea, not that I blame him after what he went through." I proceeded to tell them what Dave said about Simon working with the vampires and how Silas was most likely working for Viktor the whole time.

"I was surprised Silas could have had the forethought to send the drones if he died or we got away. It makes more sense that Viktor had that plan in place. It also shows that Viktor assumed Silas would lose, which means Viktor won't be underestimating us," Nikki said, making a very good point.

"I hadn't thought of that. I don't think that's a good thing, though," I replied.

She shook her head. "Probably not."

I took a few more drinks of blood-coffee before Nikki handed me the laptop back. "These will have everything you need. We need new phones as well for the remaining vampires. Only you and Maciah had yours on you."

"Zeke might have taken care of that already. I can check with him," Rachel said a little too quickly.

"Of course you can," I teased.

She smirked, clearly proud of what she had with Zeke. I was happy for her. We just had to find a way to help Nikki get past whatever she was feeling, and then things could level out for all of us. Well, after we killed Viktor.

I began shopping, making things easy by buying a few of the same items just in different colors. Within twenty minutes, I had a dozen outfits picked out, including underwear and shoes and a few surprises that could come in handy later.

"Anyone want to add anything before I finish this?" I offered. I knew they had some clothes here, but maybe not what they were used to.

"I'm good for now," Nikki said first, and Rachel agreed.

A few clicks and several thousand dollars later, I had a new wardrobe that was supposed to arrive within three hours. Money wasn't the most important thing in the world, but it sure did make things easier.

I leaned against the headboard, facing Rachel and Nikki. "I'm stuck in here, and shopping didn't take nearly as long as I hoped it would."

Nikki patted my leg. "We can watch movies."

"Or play board games," Rachel added.

I groaned, rubbing my hands over my face. "How long does this sun thing last?"

They both shared a look I didn't like, but it was Nikki who broke the news. "Usually two, maybe three years, but it gets easier with every day."

My skin ached just thinking about trying to ease my

way into getting used to the UV rays. That was going to make me wish I was dead.

My phone pinged with a text. I glanced at the screen to find an automated alert from my order stating my personal shopper would be acquiring all of the requested items just as soon as they opened later that morning and how much my business was appreciated. Yeah, I bet it was.

Nikki reached for the remote. "There has to be something you enjoyed watching that we can check out."

I smirked. "*Buffy the Vampire Slayer* was a favorite."

Rachel smacked me in the face with a pillow. "You're not a slayer anymore."

"Maybe not right now, but I will be again. I won't compromise on that. I know it's not safe for me to go out hunting vampires right now, but when Viktor is dead—something I have no doubt will happen soon—I'll be resuming my nightly activities."

Rachel frowned. "I know you said that before, but I hoped after some time had passed that you'd change your mind."

"That won't ever happen. Though, I'm open to doing things differently than I did before. I don't need to hunt by myself. Maciah mentioned there were other nests like yours that were too small to fight against those who didn't want things to go back to the old way, either. We could begin by helping them and spread out from there," I said.

"You'd help the other vampires, not just humans?"

Rachel asked, and the surprise in her voice hurt me a little.

"I'm okay with admitting when I'm wrong. I shouldn't have judged all vampires the same way. Helping the vampires is also helping the humans, so it's not a bad deal. Especially if more of us work together to keep the humans safe. I don't want another person to go through what I did as a teenager."

Vengeance was nothing without purpose, and I intended to make sure my purpose impacted as many people as possible for as long as I was capable of fighting for something better.

"I don't know how you're not still furious at what happened to you," Nikki said.

"Human or vampire, it doesn't matter. We all have a choice in how we feel and act. Nobody can take that from us unless we let them. I don't always succeed in keeping control of my emotions, as you've both seen, but when I've had time to process things, I can let them go if that's what is best.

"Like when Maciah didn't talk to me for six days. I didn't hold that against him, because there was no point in hurting the both of us. Making him pay wasn't going to change what happened, but it might have affected the future. I could have pushed him away and who knows what would be happening right now."

"If more people thought that way, the world would be a much easier place to live," Nikki grumbled.

My phone pinged again, and I ignored it, hoping to

get Nikki talking about what was really bothering her, but Rachel nudged me. "Um, Am? I think you'll want to see this."

I grabbed my phone from her hand and sneered at the screen.

Simon: It's a shame you weren't inside that house when I blew it up, but don't worry, I'll be seeing you soon, Amersyn. You can't hide from us.

I wanted to throw my phone across the room, but instead, I took a deep breath, taking my own advice about controlling my actions.

Me: You know I never hide, Simon. I'll be eagerly awaiting the appearance of you and the vampire friends you've made.

Hopefully, he'd take the hint that I knew exactly who he was working with.

Simon: At least my friends don't pretend to be something they're not.

I considered sending another response, but I had nothing else to say to him. He had no idea what he was talking about, but I also knew there was nothing I could say to change his mind.

The phone rang next, and it was Simon. Before I could decide if I wanted to answer, Nikki grabbed my phone from my hands and ripped it apart with little effort. "What the hell, Nik?"

"He sent a text to see if you'd respond. He made the phone call to try and track us. I'm sure of it. They must not know we left for LA already. Given we're not prepared to fight them right this minute, it's better they wait to find out where we are exactly."

Damn it. I hadn't thought of that.

"We need to destroy Maciah's phone as well. If they were trying it with mine, I'm sure they will with his, too," I said, then hesitated, unsure if I'd be able to find him where there wasn't any sun coming through the windows.

"I'll go tell him," Nikki offered and was out the door before either of us could say differently.

"We have to do something about this sun crap," I grumbled.

"We're going to Warlock tonight. Maybe we'll find someone there who will help," Rachel said with a small smile.

"Yeah, maybe." Maciah had hoped for the same thing, but I wasn't going to hold my breath.

CHAPTER 8

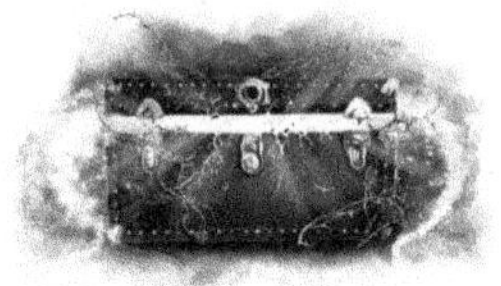

MACIAH AND ZEKE HAD TAKEN TURNS COMING INTO THE room at the worst times while we had a Marvel movie marathon. I thought I'd hate superheroes, but there was something intriguing about most of the ones in these movies. They were flawed, but they never gave up and were always trying to find humor at the darkest of times. Maybe not everything on television was utter crap.

The windows had long ago been covered, but I'd been having such a good time with Nikki and Rachel that we hadn't bothered to leave the room until it was already dark outside.

"Any thoughts on when everyone wants to head to Warlock?" Maciah asked after we'd grabbed some more servings of blood and were relaxing on the couches.

I glanced at the clock on my replacement phone that Zeke had given me earlier. He'd gone out and gotten one for each of us. It was just after nine, so only early by supernatural standards. “Sooner rather than later. If we get there before the crowds, we can see who’s coming in.”

Zeke raised his hand in the air to high-five me. “Your girl has great ideas,” he said to Maciah.

“I told him before that I was the superior decision maker, but I don’t think he believed me,” I said, slapping my palm against Zeke’s with a grin.

Maciah stared blankly at both of us, clearly not impressed. He could be such a grumpy old vampire sometimes.

My clothes had arrived in the late afternoon, so I raced up the stairs with Rachel and Nikki right on my heels. I paused at my bedroom door. “You ladies going to get dressed in my room?”

Nikki bit her lower lip. “What were you planning to wear?”

“What did you want to borrow?” I laughed, knowing they’d watched me add a few purposely chosen dresses to the cart.

Her shoulders sagged. “That gold sequin dress is stunning.”

“Good, because I bought it for you,” I said, opening my door and gesturing for her to go in first, then glanced at Rachel. “Did you happen to see something you liked?”

She threw her arms around me, squeezing tightly. “We have the best womance in the world.” Releasing me, she squealed and entered the room.

Nikki was already undressed and slipping on the dress when Rachel disappeared into my closet.

"Zip me up?" Nikki asked.

I moved her long blonde hair to the side and tugged on the zipper. "It fits perfectly."

"I needed this. Thank you," she said as Rachel came out of the closet with a satin silver piece in her grasp.

I gave Nikki's hand a squeeze, then moved my attention to Rachel.

"Was this for me?" she asked with wide eyes.

"Absolutely." I'd never given gifts to anyone before, not unless I counted the homemade ones I'd given my family over the years. Seeing how ecstatic Nikki and Rachel were, I decided that giving was something I needed to do more often.

"What are you wearing?" Nikki asked, standing in front of the mirror and running her hands over the sequins of her dress.

Without answering, I went into the closet and reached in the back for the one I'd gotten just for me. It wasn't often that I dressed up, or even wanted to, but Rachel and Nikki were breaking me down, showing me there was nothing wrong with having a little fun, even when everything was going to hell around us.

I undressed and slid the soft fabric over my head. The black dress hugged my curves, ending about mid-thigh with the smallest sequins sewn in, giving the dark fabric a shimmering appearance without being over the top. Long, loose sleeves covered my arms, and the neckline swooped just slightly beneath my neck.

The black two-inch heels I ordered were in front of

me, and I slipped those on before exiting the closet. Rachel and Nikki's grins grew simultaneously as they took in my outfit.

"Damn, girl." Nikki made a sizzling sound. "Hawt!"

Rachel nodded, bouncing on the balls of her bare feet. "We're going to have so much fun tonight."

Oh, how I hoped those weren't famous last words.

Though, instead of being a pessimist, I grinned in agreement. "Do either of you need shoes?" I asked.

"Nope. We'll meet you downstairs," Rachel said, and they took off out of my room.

I peeked in the mirror, grateful not to see bright red eyes staring back at me any longer. My ebony hair fell in thick waves down my back, and I had no makeup on, but the dress was enough to make me feel like a million dollars.

Entering the living room, my eyes roamed over Maciah's wide shoulders covered in a fitted charcoal suit jacket with a black button-up underneath. I wasn't sure where he'd gotten it from, because we'd been in the room, but I didn't care. The dark color combo accented by his sharp jawline and coffee-colored hair had me enraptured.

We met in the middle of the living room, and his hands hovered just over my arms, heating my insides without even touching me. "Utter perfection," he murmured against my cheek.

"I could say the same about you." I gripped his chin and kissed him, needing the contact before I got too worked up.

His hands splayed over my lower back and ass, pulling me flush against him. "Are you sure you want to go to Warlock?"

"We have the rest of our lives to enjoy each other, but not until Viktor is dead," I said with a bit of regret.

The sound of a lamp crashing onto the living room rug had us pulling apart just in time to see a flash of silver and black disappear down the hallway.

Nikki laughed. "Man, I knew Zeke and Rachel would be entertaining together, but I didn't expect them to have no self-control."

"Vampires. What can you do?" I joked, taking Maciah's hand and leading him toward the door.

He slowed our steps. "Are we leaving without them?"

"Rachel will be out in just a moment." I knew my friend. She wasn't going to let Zeke embarrass her in front of all of us, but she'd enjoy the private moment for a few seconds.

Sure enough, as I opened the front door, Rachel appeared at my side.

"Everything good?" I asked jokingly.

She glared for a second, then wiped all emotion from her face. "Of course."

Zeke was behind us, grumbling about womance and other things I didn't bother to catch.

Eddie, Nick, and Gabe were waiting out front, and all three were dressed in Henleys and dark jeans. Maciah nodded at Eddie, and the three of them got into the first waiting SUV while the rest of us moved toward the Range Rover we'd driven back from the airport.

Rachel, Nikki, and I sat in the back while the guys took the front as usual. It was something small we could do to make Nikki feel less left out. She was in a great mood since putting on the dress, and I'd do whatever I could to make sure the rest of her night was enjoyable as well.

Just after ten, we pulled up to Warlock. Gregory was out front, and I grimaced, remembering how I'd almost killed him. The fact that he hadn't let the fae destroy me still made no sense. Regardless, I wasn't sure how excited he'd be to see us show up.

We got out of the car, letting the valet take care of parking it out back for us. Gregory saw Zeke first, then his eyes landed on me and Maciah, appraising every inch of me with narrowed eyes.

He nodded at me as we slowed our steps. "I see you've settled well into your new life."

"I have. Thank you for your help before," I replied.

"Let's not mention it," he said, and I couldn't be more glad about that.

Zeke led the way inside with Rachel at his side. They were holding hands, and she leaned her head on his shoulder as they walked. It was freaking adorable.

We took a table in the back, facing the entry just how I preferred. I saw Eddie, Nick, and Gabe come in next, but they didn't come toward us. They ventured toward the bar, taking a seat there instead.

"Where is Jazz?" I asked. I hadn't realized until then that he was the only one who hadn't come with us.

"He's taking the loss of our nest pretty hard. His younger brother was the one lying next to them in the gym, the one who didn't make it right at the end," Zeke said.

Mother eff. I couldn't imagine. I felt for him and thought of how I'd lost my brother. I didn't blame Jazz for staying away. I might have done the same, but I'd been living in grief for years now. I knew the only way forward was to keep forcing myself to get up and move. Not move on or forget those lost—that could never happen—but to still live for myself, and them as well.

I glanced at the door to my left, remembering the last time we were here. A smile crept up my face as I pictured the shocked look on Rigo's face when I put a stake through the bastard's chest. Hopefully, he and Dmitri were both rotting in hell together.

"Is that Beatrix?" Rachael asked.

I remembered that name from the last time we were here. In fact, I had her number in my phone…which I no longer had, thanks to Nikki destroying it earlier.

"It is," Maciah said, watching the old witch waltz across the bar without a care in the world.

"Who is she, exactly?" I asked.

"A crazy, powerful witch you don't want on your bad side. She is vengeful and takes joy from testing magic on other people, but when she wants to be helpful, she's a great person to have at your side," Zeke answered.

I raised a brow at his detailed description. "Sounds like you have a past dealing with her."

"We worked with her once when we helped Roman and Cait, but not super closely. Most of what I know is because word tends to get around about those who don't hide what they're capable of. Beatrix loves the attention, because it makes smart people fear her and stupid people come after her."

"Why would she enjoy someone coming after her?" I would have been over the moon if people left me alone for the foreseeable future.

Zeke leaned in closer, lowering his voice. "Because she is batshit crazy."

A stream of light-blue magic slammed into Zeke's shoulder, and Maciah did his best to hold in a laugh. I was on my feet, ready to defend us, if necessary, but had no clue what had just happened.

Beatrix approached our table wearing navy-blue linen pants and a loose black top. Her greying hair was flowing freely behind her as if there was wind blowing around us.

"You know, vampire, I don't mind when people talk about me. So long as they're speaking the truth, and you were not. I am not crazy," she said, laying her hand on the table and smirking at Zeke with piercing eyes.

Yeah, everything about her said *crazy*, but I wasn't going to say anything. I was capable of learning from Zeke's mistakes.

Her head snapped up as she appraised me. I was the

only one at the table standing with my hands out and ready to fight.

"Were you going to do something?" she asked.

"I would have to protect my friends," I replied, keeping my tone even.

She nodded stiffly, then took a seat without being invited and gave Maciah her full attention. "Now, tell me why you're here when there are vampires out there that are ready to take your head at first sight?"

CHAPTER 9

I SAT BACK IN MY SEAT, CURIOUS AS TO HOW MACIAH planned to answer the witch. I liked that she got straight to the point. Though, she could be a bit more discreet with her execution. I caught a few heads glancing our way that I didn't care for.

"We're not hiding from this, Beatrix. If that's an inconvenience to you, I don't know what you want me to do about it," Maciah said.

She thrummed her fingers on the table, glancing over each of us before settling back on Maciah. "What's your plan?"

Maciah smirked. "Why would I tell you?"

I tensed, assuming she'd react badly to his cocky attitude. Instead, she laughed. "I'm not sure. Maybe you want my help?"

Even if she was missing a few screws, help wasn't a bad idea, but Maciah shut her down.

"No, thanks. We have things handled," he said casually.

Her lips thinned, telling me she wasn't used to being told no. I wasn't sure that Maciah was making the right move, but I trusted him to know what was best.

Beatrix pushed back in the chair. "Okay, then." She stood up slowly, still watching Maciah, but his poker face was on point.

The witch turned and took a few steps back toward the bar, but she spun around again, glaring at Maciah. "Seriously?"

He merely shrugged.

Beatrix huffed and crossed her arms, then moved her stare to me. "Come here."

"I'm good right here," I said, but Maciah pulled my chair out with one hand.

"Go ahead."

My gaze moved between him and the witch. "What is happening?"

"Trust me," he murmured, then nudged me to get up.

I did as he asked and walked toward the witch. She appraised me, then inhaled deeply. "You don't smell like Junie anymore. That's disappointing."

"I died. I'm not going to apologize for that," I deadpanned.

She winked. "No, you probably shouldn't. You do need my help, though."

My brow raised. "Do I? I don't remember asking for it."

"You didn't." She pulled the fabric of my dress down far enough that she could press her palm over my chest without the material getting in the way. "Wouldn't want to ruin your outfit," she mocked, then a zap of electricity rolled through me.

My teeth clenched together, and my hands grabbed on to her arm, ready to break the contact I hadn't asked for, but the pain only lasted for a second until warmth replaced the ache.

Magic moved along my skin, awakening the power I'd kept locked down since we found the others alive. There hadn't been any reason to use the mind control since then. The energy had been peacefully stagnant until the witch began poking at things that didn't need poking.

"Enough," I snarled.

She smirked. "I know. I was just seeing how far I could push you. What are you hiding inside there?"

"Nothing that concerns you," I snapped, annoyed at her tactics.

Beatrix peered around me, nodding at Maciah. "I see why you two were meant for each other. Is my show of good faith enough for you? I'm frustrated with another task and could use a distraction. Plus, I have something that could help you."

I moved away from the witch and back to the other side of the table. I wasn't sure what good faith she was talking about, but clearly, she and Maciah had a silent conversation I'd completely missed.

Rachel leaned in closer and whispered, "Maciah

doesn't trust very easily. Beatrix just made it so you can be in the sun as proof she's not trying to screw with us."

Well, that was nice of her. I suddenly felt bad for calling her crazy.

She winked at me a second time, then reclaimed her seat. "So, what are we dealing with?"

Again, I never heard Maciah agree to working with her, but she seemed pretty certain that problem was dealt with.

"Viktor Cross. He screwed up seven years ago and now he's trying to rectify that by hiring other vampires to kill Amersyn. Only they've all failed, and I have a feeling time is running out for the vampire to complete this particular task," Maciah said quietly.

The mention of Viktor having messed up seven years ago caused my chest to twist in a way it hadn't in weeks. I tried not to think about the fact that I was the reason vampires had attacked my family. I knew there was nothing I could do to change the past, so my motto was not to dwell on it, but when the event was brought up unexpectedly…sometimes I couldn't control my emotions.

Maciah reached for me, likely sensing my distress. I tried to offer him a smile, but one never came.

"I have one of Viktor's men locked up. He could be helpful," Beatrix said.

Zeke shook his head. "We're not negotiating with Viktor, and we don't have the resources to keep an eye on a hostage."

Beatrix smiled in a serial killer sort of way. "He wouldn't need to be a hostage. I've spent a decent amount of time working to reform Dante."

The way she said "reform" had me believing this witch enjoyed torturing people much more than she did helping them.

"Dante Rhodes?" Nikki asked.

"The one and only. He chose the wrong area to go on a blood binge, leaving me no choice but to deal with him," Beatrix said.

"How did you get him?" Rachel asked next.

"I hired Lucinda Morrow. She used to be the type not to ask questions as long as she knew someone deserved to be punished. She's not as fun anymore now that she fell in love." Beatrix seemed truly put out by that fact.

Maciah still wasn't liking the idea of taking the vampire. We had enough to deal with, and there was no way to trust Beatrix had truly changed someone who once worked for Viktor.

"We can't take Dante off your hands, but if you're willing to offer anything else, we're happy to talk," Maciah said.

Beatrix leaned back in her chair and crossed her arms. "You're a stubborn vampire, but it's understandable given how your nest just blew up. I really do need the distraction, so it's your lucky day. I'm going to help you, and maybe in the future, if I need assistance, you won't hesitate to do so."

Ah, there it was. Rarely did people give without

expecting something in return. While annoying, in this instance, it wasn't the worst thing.

"We can offer help from myself and Maciah in the future, but not our whole nest. We've already lost too much. That's either good enough, or we're done here," I said when the pause grew uncomfortably long.

The witch grinned at me, wrinkles forming around her face. "I like you. We've got a deal."

Nikki and Rachel were glaring at me, but I wasn't willing to risk losing them again, and I could feel the pride building within Maciah. I'd made the right decision to speak up.

"So, with that being said, you're welcome to come with me to my place once I'm done here," Beatrix said.

Zeke's eyes widened. "To your coven?"

She smirked. "Absolutely not. Nobody knows where my witches sleep, but I'm confident enough in my magic to show you where I do business. You could even have a little chat with Dante while you're there."

Maybe that was something we needed to consider for the future. A nest that nobody knew about. In case psychotic vampires wanted to blow up our home again. Mother-effing bloodsuckers.

The witch got up from the table and walked away without another word. She disappeared into the crowd somehow, even though the place wasn't full yet.

"Do you trust her?" I asked Maciah.

"I think she has an agenda, but she won't do anything to piss me off to the point I would consider her an enemy. She gets a thrill out of pushing people. I just have to do my best not to react when she pokes. Working with her will be helpful in keeping everyone safer."

I knew he was worried about the remaining members of his nest. After losing as many as we did, it wasn't easy to accept.

Nikki leaned in closer. "What about Dante? Do you really think Beatrix broke him?"

Zeke chuckled. "I think that witch could break anyone. You do realize who she is, right?"

"Of course, but Dante Rhodes was one of Viktor's top vampires for a reason," Nikki said defensively.

"We're going to be leery of him. Nikki is right, but so is Zeke. Let's not talk about that anymore tonight and see what we can learn while we wait for Beatrix to finish her business," Maciah said, and I was glad to see his support of Nikki's concern. While I didn't know of Dante, I had no desire to let him into our home or trust he would willingly give us information that would help us defeat a man he used to kill for.

"Should we split up?" Rachel suggested.

"That's not a bad idea, as long as we can still see each other," I said.

"Nikki, you'll go to the bar. Rachel and Zeke on the dance floor while me and Amersyn take a stroll around the room once or twice," Maciah said, pushing back his chair.

I moved to do the same, but he had already done so. I

smiled at him as I stood up from the table, settling my hand in his offered palm.

Rachel was beaming as Zeke twirled her onto the dance floor. The music was on a completely different beat, but that didn't matter to the two of them. Not when they had each other.

I turned to see Maciah wiping a hand over his mouth. "Were you just smiling?" I asked.

"Am I not allowed to do that?" he countered.

I narrowed my eyes. "You are, but you rarely do it for anyone other than me. I need an explanation. What did I miss?"

"Nothing. We were both watching the same thing," he said with a shrug.

I squeezed his hand. "I know you explained why you stopped openly caring about the vampires, but you don't have to hide your feelings from me. I hope you know that."

Maciah pressed his lips to my forehead. "Some habits are harder to break than others."

Wasn't that the truth, but it was good to see that Maciah was truly happy for Zeke and Rachel. Even if he never told them that with words, I hoped they could sense it.

Though, I didn't fault Maciah for struggling with his ways. There wasn't much difference between him and the old me. He'd let people in, trying to save as many as he could, all while keeping them at arm's length. I'd just slammed the door in everyone's face, trying to kill as many as I could.

Okay, maybe we weren't the same at all in that aspect, but our reasonings were similar.

Still, if I could change, I knew Maciah could as well.

CHAPTER 10

WE SPENT TWENTY MINUTES CIRCLING THE CLUB, GOING AS far as we could without losing sight of the others. The only suspicious thing we'd found was a wolf shifter just a few barstools away from Nikki. He wasn't bothering anyone, but he wasn't okay, either.

"Care to dance?" I asked Maciah since Beatrix hadn't reappeared.

He tensed for a moment, then nodded. "Only for you."

He didn't twirl me onto the dance floor, but his hands held me in a way that had me wishing we were alone instead of in a room full of people. His left was splayed over my lower back and the right held my hand, keeping them pressed between us as we swayed to the slower beat.

Our eyes locked, and the shared magic we had warmed my chest, reminding me that the energy I wasn't used to was no longer dormant, thanks to Beatrix messing with me. Though, I wasn't going to be upset about that if I really could be out in the sun without waiting years for it to happen naturally.

With every full turn we made, our bodies pressed closer and closer together. Even though we weren't at Warlock to have a night off, I appreciated this moment with Maciah and didn't take it for granted.

All of a sudden, though, a shock rolled through him and ended inside me, unleashing the power I had no use for. My jaw tensed, and I had to close my eyes before I revealed to anyone close to us what I was capable of.

Maciah spun around, keeping me at his side, and both of us sneered when I reopened my eyes. The energy was settling over my tingling skin, but that wasn't good enough for me. Not when there were so many people around us that didn't know who I was.

"Beatrix," Maciah growled.

"I'm done. We can leave," she said as if she'd done nothing wrong, then added, "Actually, one more thing."

As I forced my heir power back into its box, Beatrix walked toward the bar and straight to the wolf shifter we'd been eyeballing. I tugged on Maciah's hand once I had more control. I wanted to be close enough to see what interest the witch had in the lone shifter.

"Why are you still here?" Beatrix asked him.

"Because I have to be," he snarled.

She sighed. "If you'd just tell me what you're looking for, maybe I could help."

"Your version of help is pointing me toward a pack of wolves I'm not needed at. My mate isn't with them. I know it," the wolf said, losing the bite in his tone as he mentioned a mate.

Maciah pulled me away, and we went to Nikki.

"We're leaving," Maciah said as Rachel and Zeke joined us.

"I'll tell them to bring the car up," Zeke said, and Rachel went with him.

Nikki glanced at the shifter, then back at us. "Everything good?"

"Yeah. That wolf isn't here for trouble," Maciah said.

"Did you hear anything interesting while you were sitting up here?" I asked Nikki.

She shrugged. "Not really. A few people talking about a supernatural party at some mansion. Some more going on about the weather. Some talk about Lucinda showing up again. Apparently, she's a big deal around here."

"Only because she's the only fae to live away from the islands for so long. Or at least to publicly do so," Maciah answered, clearly not impressed with the fae.

I had only talked to her for a minute and while recovering from almost killing Gregory, but she seemed like someone I could get along with. Especially since her first instinct was to kill me. Yeah, that was twisted, but I was the same way. Maybe I'd get to meet her under better circumstances one day.

Beatrix came back over when she was done with the wolf, and she didn't look pleased.

"Trouble in paradise?" I asked, wanting to know more about the guy. Something about him piqued my interest.

She huffed. "No, only a stubborn male who thinks he knows best, regardless of what other people tell him."

"What's his name?" I asked as we headed toward the exit.

"Foster. Foster pain-in-my-ass Kline."

"Did something happen to his mate?" Nikki asked.

Beatrix glared at nothing. "He doesn't even know who she is, but apparently, his wolf says that he can feel she's here. Something that shouldn't even be possible. Even the local alpha doesn't understand. Though, he's sent all his available females near the rogue wolf and none of them have a connection to Foster."

That had Maciah's attention. "Maybe he's not mated to a wolf."

"I have a feeling you're right, and that's not the kind of attention we need around here. Not when I have other problems to deal with."

We walked out the door to find both of our SUVs already waiting, with Gabe, Eddie, and Nick already loaded into the first one.

Gregory was still working the entrance, and I waved goodbye to him. He tossed a nod our way before giving his attention to the line that was now curving around the side of the building to get in, mostly filled with humans who would probably never get in. As far as I knew, humans only got in for special events that very few knew about, like Rigo's party.

Beatrix moved ahead of us, sliding into the passenger seat without asking then closing the door.

"Seriously? Who does that witch think she is?" Nikki asked.

"Someone who has more power than she should," Maciah grumbled, then headed to speak to Eddie who had the passenger window rolled down on the other vehicle, waiting for us.

Our Range Rover had three rows, so Zeke regretfully got into the very back while Rachel, Nikki, and I slid into the middle while we waited on Maciah.

"No car for you to worry about?" Nikki asked Beatrix.

"Nope, and I can't give directions from the back, so here I am," she said, as if that justified her actions.

Maciah got in and sighed when he saw Beatrix sitting next to him instead of one of us. "I sent the others back to the house to check on Jazz." Then, he started the SUV and pulled away from the club. The air around us was thick with tension, but for once, I wasn't worried. Beatrix was brash, but it felt right, as if we should have been working with her all along.

"Turn left here, then make your second right," Beatrix said.

I could see Maciah's hands flex over the leather steering wheel. He seemed to be barely tolerating the witch, but hopefully once she gave us something more helpful, he would ease up some.

Beatrix continued with her directions, sometimes even seeming to take us in circles, but we finally pulled into an empty driveway of a standard suburban home. This might not be where her coven resided, but it still wasn't what I expected with its white picket fence, perfectly manicured lawn, and puffs of smoke coming out of the chimney.

We got out of the car and headed toward the gate. Beatrix stood in front of it with her hand out. "You need to touch my palm first before you pass through."

"Why?" I asked.

"Do you want to find out for yourself?" she countered with a gleam in her eyes.

No, I really didn't. I placed my hand on hers first. There was a zap of something that didn't hurt like she'd done to me earlier, but it wasn't pleasant.

I looked up to find a completely different house in front of us. "Did you teleport us?"

"No. The house you saw is an illusion with perfectly crafted spells to keep the unwanted out and the wanted in. Now, who's next?"

Maciah went next, followed by the rest of our group. As they finished up, I took in the magic that I could now feel pulsing around me, pressing down against my skin and making me feel energized.

The real house was a three-story home with pristine dark-grey siding and white trim that matched the picket fence I could still see. All of the windows had light shining through them, making me think there were more than a handful of witches filling the house.

Beatrix led us through the small gate once everyone

had touched her hand. Before I followed her into the house, I glanced behind us, feeling like someone was there.

All I saw was an opaque shimmering shield and another SUV passing by that was probably just headed home.

Beatrix grabbed my arm. "You're safe here. I promise."

That was the first nice thing she'd said to me. Even still, I believed her.

"What happens if a kid throws a ball over your fence by accident and tries to enter?" I asked, hoping she wasn't a potential threat to harmless children.

"If any human crosses the shield, they get disoriented, turn around, and forget what they were doing. All while realizing they now have a minor headache and need to head home before it gets worse," Beatrix said proudly.

"What about a supernatural?" Maciah asked.

Beatrix grinned. "That's my little secret. Now, how about we go check out what I have that might help?"

Inside was homey. Candles were lit all around us, casting light on the different-colored walls. Not one seemed to be the same shade. Oddly enough, the paint didn't clash.

There were stairs to our left and a living room on our right with a hallway straight ahead that appeared to curve around.

Beatrix took the stairs, and we stopped at the second floor. I'd seen three floors of windows, yet the stairs didn't continue.

"How do you get up to the next floor?" I asked.

"You're a curious vampire. Maybe not the best trait for you," she chided.

"Or maybe I don't like walking into a house that I know nothing about with a witch I don't know," I said with a smirk.

She grinned back and said nothing else. Maciah, on the other hand, pulled me to the side. "Try not to prod the witch when we're inside her house, please."

I patted him on the chest. "Only because you said *please* will I stop being nosy."

"I'm not saying thank you for that," he grumbled before moving ahead.

Rachel and Nikki came to my side. "You really don't have any fear, do you?" Nikki asked.

"I do. I just don't let the emotion dictate what I do or don't do," I replied.

"I want to argue with that, but I've got nothing," Rachel said, and Nikki nodded.

"Same."

We hurried across the dark wood floors and caught up with the guys. Beatrix had her back to them and was digging through shelves while muttering incoherent words to herself.

"Should we be worried?" Rachel asked.

Zeke put an arm around her. "Not yet."

"Where's Dante?" Maciah asked with a raised voice.

Beatrix bumped her head as she backed away from the

cabinet. "It's not necessary to yell. I might be old, but I'm not senile."

Yeah, I definitely liked her.

"Apologies," Maciah said, but didn't sound one bit sincere.

Beatrix fumbled with some bottles she was pulling from her pockets. "I thought you didn't want to hassle with Dante?"

"That doesn't mean I might not want to see him," Maciah answered.

"Hmmm," was all she said in reply before diving back into the cabinet.

This time, she had nearly half her body inside the dark space, which shouldn't have been possible from the size I could see, but then again, why wouldn't her potion cabinet be magically bigger and probably protected?

The five of us waited silently for another few minutes before Beatrix's head popped back out. She turned toward us, blowing a strand of grey hair out of her face, and set the additional bottles down.

"I don't like to give out my magic often, but more than that, I don't like Viktor. I'd prefer him dead after what he did to Dante," she said, her hands curving protectively around the dozen or so bottles in front of her.

"Did the vampire grow on you since you captured him?" Zeke asked.

"No, but I'm not a heartless witch, either. I forced him to tell me everything I wanted to know, and it wasn't pretty, but none of it was a lie. Viktor is the worst of your kind, and I know the world you all are trying to build for your vampires. All supernaturals would be better off with more vampires like you around."

Zeke and even Maciah were stunned by her words, but there wasn't a moment to appreciate them before the witch opened her mouth again.

"So, don't screw this up and make me regret helping you. As I said, I don't like to waste magic."

Ah, there was the snarky witch I was getting used to.

"We'll do our best," I said so Maciah didn't have to pretend he wasn't ready to rip her head off.

CHAPTER 11

BEATRIX SIGHED HEAVILY. "WERE YOU EVEN PAYING attention for the last five minutes? *This* is stun and *that* is a bomb. Quite the opposite of each other."

Her potions were colored very similarly, making it hard to remember which was what, but she insisted each of us had to get them all right before she'd relinquish the magic to us.

"Okay, I got it. Stun and bomb. I won't confuse them again," Zeke said. He'd gotten the rest of them correct, at least.

Maciah, Rachel, and I had already passed Beatrix's test and Nikki had yet to go, but it seemed we were going to get lucky.

"I don't have the patience for you people anymore." She shoved the bottles into a drawstring bag, then handed them to me. "Don't be an idiot with these."

I wanted to pop back at her with something snarky,

but we were almost done. I didn't want her to take the potions back, because there was no doubt in my mind that they'd help with our fight against Viktor. He might be too strong from my mental abilities, but Beatrix's magic was potent.

There was even a delusion one that sounded like a lot of fun.

"If you want to see Dante still, he's in the basement," Beatrix said as we stepped onto the stairs.

She led the way to the modest kitchen. There were three other witches in there, but before we could really look at them, Beatrix was ushering us forward. "Hurry up before my patience really runs out."

Maciah went down the second set of stairs first. The magic became heavier with every step we took, running along my skin almost as if it was tasting me.

"He's in the corner," Beatrix said and pointed.

The space was all concrete and wood beams with no life, unlike the main part of the house. I turned to where the witch had gestured, shocked to see that there was nothing keeping the vampire locked up. I knew she'd said he was reformed, but still…I wouldn't have trusted him in my house.

His eyes were darker than Maciah's with streaks of red bleeding through them, getting brighter the longer he glared at us. There were circles under his eyes, and his lips thinned beneath his crooked nose.

"I thought you said he was reformed?" Zeke asked.

"If you'd have seen him before, you'd agree. The only

time that vampire was calm prior to me getting a hold of him was when he thought he was going to get lucky and needed to keep up appearances," Beatrix said.

"What are they doing here?" Dante asked.

"They're trying to kill Viktor. I thought you could give them something useful," Beatrix replied with a forced smile.

Dante laughed darkly. "Nobody can get close enough to Viktor to kill him."

"We don't have to get close to him. He's going to come to us," Maciah said, and I hoped that was true. Going to Silas had resulted in one too many surprises for me to want to repeat that tactic.

"Well, then I wish you luck," the vampire said, almost sounding genuine. "I have nothing that can help you," he added.

I turned Maciah toward me and lowered my voice as much as I could. "I could do that thing."

"Absolutely not."

Yeah, I kind of figured that would be his answer. He was still firmly against too many people knowing about my heir powers. Plus, if Dante had been as strong as Nikki made him sound, it probably wouldn't have been worth my time or the risk of letting another person know what I was capable of.

"Thank you, Beatrix, but we're done," Maciah said.

As the five of us turned our backs on Dante, he hissed, then spoke through gritted teeth. "I might have something."

Beatrix nodded at him in approval.

"This is something I haven't even told Beatrix yet because by the time I trusted her, I didn't want her to get mixed up with Viktor. But if you're really going up against him, then you need to know, he's not a normal vampire."

"What do you mean?" Nikki asked.

"His tracking skills are the best I've ever seen. So good that I'm nearly positive they're not natural."

Beatrix grimaced. "Like he's using dark magic? From a witch?"

Dante nodded.

"Why would you think that?" Maciah asked.

"Because he keeps different supernaturals in his compound. A small pack of wolves, a few witches, and even a fae. They're not allowed to leave their rooms, and nobody but Viktor enters them. Whatever he has them for, it has to be for his own personal gain."

Everyone was quiet as we took in the information. I wasn't sure how the revelation affected us, but I knew it was never good to go against someone dealing in dark magic.

Maciah offered a stiff nod to Dante. "We'll let you know when he's dead."

"And I'm happy to stay here until that happens," Dante replied, turning to go back to the single bed behind him.

We headed back up the stairs, and the witches from

before were already gone from the kitchen. We went down another hallway and ended up in the living room.

Beatrix pointed at me. "I need you to come with me. The rest of you stay right here. If you try to sneak around my house, I will know, and you will pay."

Maciah grabbed my arm. "She's not going anywhere alone with you."

I placed my hand over his. "Would we be here if you really thought she had ill intentions toward any of us?"

He glowered at me.

"Loosen the protector hat. Beatrix won't hurt me."

She made a half-laugh, half-grunt sound from behind me, not helping the situation.

"I'll be fine," I pressed, mostly because I was curious about what she had to say. Beatrix didn't seem like the type to do things for no reason or on a whim.

Maciah's hold on my arm loosened. "Hurry back. We need to get going."

"Thank you." I spun around before he could change his mind and we ended up in a fight, because I was going with Beatrix either way.

She was waiting at the base of the stairs for me, and I followed her up. Instead of going to the same area as before, she took me into a bedroom with light pink walls, white bedding, and minimal furniture.

"This was one of Junie's rooms. She had it made for her niece Andie, but then something happened and the likelihood of Andie ever returning diminished. Junie always said she'd find her again, but there was always a reason why she hadn't yet. A decision that has left ramifications my coven needs to deal with now that Junie's no longer with us," Beatrix said.

"Why are you showing me this?" I asked curiously.

"Because Junie once thought your father, and even you, were worth saving. She was my oldest friend, and I want to finish what she started. I did some searching after I met you at Warlock the first time."

Beatrix was hinting at answers I'd been hoping to find one day. I didn't peg the witch as someone to just hand them over, but maybe I'd been wrong.

"Junie and your father were friends. A secret she kept even from me. He was the only vampire she trusted. He saved her life one time, and she returned the favor when you were born in hopes of keeping you from a life Darius never wanted for you. I can see there's no changing your path now. You were meant for this world, regardless of what Darius wanted, but I know if Junie was here, she'd help you."

I brushed hair behind my ear as I turned away from the room and toward Beatrix who was still standing next to me. "So, you're going to help me because of your friendship with Junie?"

"A little because of that, a little because I need to focus on something new, and a little because I'm curious what has you strung so tightly. Your magic isn't meant to be restrained. The vampires with you might be doing their best to help you, but they can't understand what's inside here." She placed her hand on my chest.

I was blown away that she seemed sincere with her words. She'd seemed so selfish before, but none of my internal warnings were going off, so I went with it.

"So, you do understand what's inside me. How can you help?" I asked.

I followed her as the witch walked back toward the area we'd been before and reopened her cabinet. "If Viktor is really meddling with dark magic, you're going to need to understand the power inside you in order to counter what he's been working with for years."

Beatrix opened a drawer and pulled out a vial of clear, thick liquid.

"What's that?" I asked immediately, already knowing she was going to ask me to drink it.

"Something to loosen you up." The grin on her face told me everything I didn't want to know.

As much as I wanted to refuse, I also wanted answers. Ones that even Maciah couldn't give me, no matter how much he wanted to. There was too much unknown about the original vampires. Too much about me that didn't line up with history books. We needed to do whatever it took to find the answers we needed to beat Viktor.

Only then could we relax and have the life we deserved.

I snatched the bottle from Beatrix's hand and popped the cork off. "I'm supposed to drink this, yeah?" I didn't figure it was smart to assume anything when it came to magic.

"Well, you're not putting it up your pooper," she replied, and I nearly dropped the vial from shock.

At first, no sounds left me, but then my laughter bubbled to the surface. It was real and not forced and exactly what I needed.

I reined in my chuckles and downed the contents in one gulp, surprised it tasted like sugar and not garbage.

Beatrix took the vial from me and pointed to a chair. "Sit there until you start to float."

"Seriously?"

She rolled her eyes. "No, Amersyn. You can't float. You're a vampire. But you're going to be unsteady on your feet in about thirty seconds. Now, sit."

She pushed me into the chair, and I sat with an umph. My skin had goosebumps, and my hair began rising around me like there was static calling the strands up. I glanced above me, looking for something, but instead, it appeared as if the roof was growing taller.

My arms moved out to my sides, trying to steady myself, and a heavy beating pulsed in my chest. I looked down, expecting to see something there, but it was only my dress.

My feet came up in front of me, and I glared at the heels I'd worn. What had I been thinking? I preferred boots to heels any day.

Wait. Why was I in heels? Where was I? What was I supposed to be doing? The lights in the room dimmed, and I whipped my head around, trying to see who was there and what they wanted.

Then, a realization that should have frightened me but didn't settled over me: I didn't even know who I was. Was I supposed to be concerned with someone else there? Was I in danger?

As my pulse quickened, sharp points poked at my lower lip. I rubbed a finger over them, only to come back with blood coating my skin. Using my tongue, I did a once-over on my teeth. *Fangs? No, not possible.*

But as I said the word, I knew it was. Fangs. Blood. Vampire.

I was a vampire.

Yes, that was true, but I still didn't know what I was doing or where I was.

"Look inside yourself, Amersyn," a woman's voice whispered near my ear.

I turned toward the sound, but nothing was there and the light in the room faded away faster by the second.

I closed my eyes and did as the voice suggested. It was a voice I knew I was supposed to know but couldn't place. Inside me, there was light. It was white and full of energy. It weaved through my veins like fire raging in a forest. I reached to touch the wisps with my mind, but as I got closer, they moved further away from me.

I scrunched my face, following after the trail until it ended at a box. There was no more light, only darkness and a wooden chest that rocked back and forth.

I backed away from the chest, unsure if it should be opened.

"Not opened, but destroyed," the same voice whispered.

Destroyed? I couldn't do that. Could I?

There was a part of me hesitating, but I didn't understand why. I trusted the voice. At least, I was pretty sure I did.

As heat crept up my spine, my instincts screamed at me that I didn't have any other choice. If I didn't listen to the voice, then things were going to get worse. I just didn't know if it would be worse for me or for the voice.

Regardless, I ignored the concerned part of me and rammed my metaphorical fist into the imaginary chest, hoping I hadn't just made a mistake that would cost me more than I was willing to pay.

CHAPTER 12

THE WHITE WISPS I'D PREVIOUSLY SEEN EXPLODED INTO A frenzy of tornadoes as they whipped with intensity inside me, throwing me off balance as I dug my nails into the chair I was sitting in. A wave of nausea churned in my stomach, but I gritted my teeth and held on tightly, trying to fight off any negative effects.

The burning that had previously begun in my spine, spread out and covered every inch of my skin, but not severe like fire, more like I'd been laying under the sun for much too long. Then, everything began to itch, but my grip was locked down, unable to move from the chair.

"Almost done," the voice whispered. This time, there was some glee coming from the woman.

I pushed through my memories. Everything was foggy, but I knew they were there. I just had to force them back to me. I lashed out at the white wisps swirling through me, trying to find my way back to myself.

I was strong and capable. Whatever this was, it wasn't meant to overpower me. I was meant to control it. I knew that deep in my soul.

A throaty scream built inside me, and I released it like a banshee. Only, the sound never left my mouth. It merely echoed around my mind, rattling my bones until the energy inside me began calming.

Not just calming but getting smaller.

I tried to reach for the wisps, but they began attaching themselves to my insides, disappearing wherever they could.

As soon as there was no other light bouncing around within me, my fingers released the arms of the chair, and my eyes cracked open.

I was in Beatrix's house. She gave me a potion. She helped me. Again.

I remembered everything as soon as I opened my eyes. The witch was sitting across from me with her ankles crossed and a smirk on her face.

"Better?" she asked.

A part of me really wanted to snap back at her, but I took a second to consider her question. The chest I'd locked the original power in was gone. My body felt stronger, more powerful than should be allowed. Almost as if I could destroy everything in my path.

"I didn't want this power," I said.

I didn't want to be capable of destruction. I didn't want people to seek me out because of what I was given from my ancestors. I didn't want the responsibility that came with being this powerful.

"And that's exactly why you have it. You're different for a reason. Junie knew that, and I know it now. You unlocked your powers by bonding with Maciah as your protector, but they weren't properly dispersed. No vampire before you has been capable of what you are. You needed a little magic to make things right."

My hands roamed over my arms and thighs. There was an electrical charge everywhere I touched, but it wasn't like before. I remembered Rachel telling me that the power wasn't separate from me. I'd thought she was wrong, considering how I could lock it up.

Now that it was embedded in my body, I knew what she meant. We just hadn't known how to make that happen before Beatrix inserted herself into my life.

"Thank you," I said to her, hoping to convey the sincerity I was feeling.

I'd felt lost for a long time. Even more so since finding out that I was going to be a vampire…and then becoming one. Maciah had helped, along with the others, but there had still been an uncertainty simmering inside me that I had done my best to ignore.

Beatrix had blown that doubt to shreds with one vial of magic.

"I owed it to Junie to see this through for her. Like I said, she was my oldest friend. I don't have too many of those in this world. You'll learn it's good to hold on to the good ones when you find them."

Was this snarky witch getting soft on me? I was tempted to call her out but decided better of it. We might still need her help.

"Sounds like you were lucky to have each other for the time that you did," I said, standing up from the chair. "I should probably get back downstairs before Maciah comes storming up."

Beatrix smirked, back to her normal self. "Or you could make him wait. Might be fun."

I laughed. "I agree, but we're running tight on time. We have no idea where Viktor is, and we don't want to be unprepared when we find out."

She got up as well and placed her hand on my shoulder. "Just remember who you are, Amersyn. No matter what, you're still the same woman you were prior to meeting Maciah. Your punch just packs more power than before."

I nodded, placing my hand over hers. "I will. I promise. Viktor won't stand a chance against us."

That was something I fully believed as long as he didn't catch us by surprise.

"That's the way to think. Now, go on. Like you said, time isn't on your side."

We headed back downstairs to find Nikki looking out the window, Zeke and Rachel on the loveseat, and Maciah pacing around the room.

Our eyes locked, then his gaze moved over me, checking for injuries, or so I assumed. "You're okay."

I nodded. "Better than before."

"There's no better witch than me," Beatrix added as she brushed past me.

A small smirk played on my lips, and I shook my head at the witch's confidence before heading to see what had Nikki's attention. She wasn't moving from the window, which raised a red flag for me.

"Everything okay?" I asked when I stood next to her.

"Not sure. Something just feels off."

"It's probably the shield around the house. Makes some people feel trapped," Beatrix said, grabbing the bag I'd left on the table and shoving it toward me. "Don't forget these. You might feel more powerful, but you're going to need all of the help you can get."

I took the bag and grabbed Maciah's hand. We followed Rachel and Zeke to the door with Nikki right behind us.

An SUV passed slowly, and Nikki tensed. "I've seen that same one three times since we've been here."

It was also the vehicle I'd seen when we arrived.

"Do you know them?" Maciah asked Beatrix as she moved to peek out the door, too.

She shook her head. "Never seen it around here. As long as you stay on the property, even the driveway, they can't see you."

Rachel and Zeke were already on the porch and stepped onto the yard instead of going out the front gate. As the rest of us stepped out, the vehicle stopped, leaving the engine still running.

I followed our friends with Maciah and Nikki at my

side. We got halfway across the grass to join Rachel and Zeke before the car doors opened.

Two men stepped out—only one of which I recognized from his widow's peak and beady eyes.

"Viktor," Maciah hissed next to me.

Beatrix appeared at our side. "They won't be able to see or hear you."

I wasn't sure she was right, but maybe it was only a coincidence that they'd gotten out of the SUV just as soon as we stepped outside.

Zeke stepped back to speak with Maciah, and I joined Rachel's side at the edge of the yard with Nikki right next to me as well.

The three of us linked arms as I kept the bag of potions held in front of me, waiting with bated breath to see what Viktor had planned. Four more vampires got out of the vehicle, but Viktor snapped his fingers and they got back inside.

At least we knew how many we were dealing with in case Beatrix's shield wasn't as good as she believed.

Viktor sniffed the air and stepped closer. "I can smell the power in your blood, Amersyn. It calls to me."

His Russian accent wasn't strong, but I could still hear it within his words as he spoke to me.

Maciah was gripping my shoulders the moment after Viktor used my name. "He won't touch you," Maciah grumbled in my ear.

Viktor stepped closer, his hands inching closer to the opaque shield, and he inhaled once more, closing his eyes as he did only to open them and stare directly at me. "I will have you, Amersyn. You can't hide with the witches forever. You're my prize to collect, and I always get what I want."

I shuddered, creeped out that his beady red eyes seemed to be piercing right through my soul, regardless of Beatrix's shield.

His tongue flicked out, licking his lips. "And such a prize to be had."

Maciah snarled, then tried to break through the arm I had linked with Rachel, but Zeke was right there and prepared. He had arms wrapped around Maciah before he could leap through the shield and do something we weren't prepared for.

"He's not going to touch her. I won't let him have her," Maciah hissed, and I went to him as Viktor headed for his vehicle again.

I placed both of my hands on Maciah's face, forcing him to focus on me instead of Viktor's retreating form. "I'm right here. We're together and nobody is going to change that. I promise you."

Maciah took a deep breath, his chest rising and falling rapidly. "He needs to die."

"I know, and he will. Soon. We just need to have our team together before that happens," I said softly.

He nodded, and Zeke released him. Maciah turned to Beatrix. "You've already helped more than we expected—I can feel the changes in Amersyn—but we need one more favor."

She raised a greying brow. "And that would be?"

"Can you put one of these shields around my property? As much as I prefer that Viktor comes to us, having something in place to make sure we're not taken by surprise would be helpful."

Beatrix watched Viktor's vehicle drive away and crossed her arms, drumming her fingers. "I can, but you're going to owe me big. I have a problem I'm working on, and I might need you to track someone down for me."

Maciah's brow pinched. "You're a witch. Can't you do a tracking spell?"

She narrowed her eyes on him. "Don't question me, Vampire."

"Okay, fine. You'll be the first person we see when this is over," Maciah answered.

"I promise I'll hold him to that," I added.

Beatrix grinned. "I know."

She spun around and headed for our Range Rover, once again getting into the front seat.

"Should we leave here so soon? Viktor could be waiting just around the corner," Rachel said, making a valid point.

"I'm sure Beatrix has a plan," I said. Hopefully, I wasn't wrong about that.

We got into the car, taking the same seats as before. As soon as all of the doors were closed, Beatrix turned to face us. "Don't throw up."

Then, she placed her hands on the dashboard and

closed her eyes. The glow of magic grew around her until sparks formed and everything surrounding us disappeared. The car wobbled and then dropped like a roller coaster ride before tilting from one side to the other.

I tried to see out the windows, but there was nothing other than blackness beyond the glass. Beatrix's magic was the only light around us.

A few seconds later, her light dimmed, only to be replaced by the moonlight above us. Maciah's LA house came into view as well. Eddie and Nick were on the porch with confused faces as we got out of the car.

Eddie was at Maciah's door in the next second, opening it up. "What the hell was that?"

Maciah nodded at Beatrix. "A favor."

Beatrix got out of the vehicle first and walked down the long driveway. "Don't follow me," she called as I took a step after her.

Well, okay then. I turned to face Rachel as she got out of the SUV on my side. She wasn't smiling, and I didn't like to see her so stressed.

"Everything is going to be fine," I said, but as the words left my mouth, a shadow whipped past us and around the back of the house.

"What was that?" I asked.

Maciah, Eddie, and Zeke were already standing next to each other, arms out and ready for a fight. Beatrix didn't come running back, so I wasn't overly worried, but she also might have missed whoever snuck onto the property.

"Stay here," Maciah said before the three of them disappeared.

Yeah, that didn't really work for me, but I wasn't going to chase immediately after them in case more vampires were out there. "Come on," I said to Nikki and Rachel before tossing the bag of potions over my shoulder.

"You know when someone usually says everything is going to be fine, that's when everything blows up in our face. Maybe don't say that again," Nikki said as we moved to the front of the house where Nick was still waiting.

"Yeah, maybe."

Rachel was still quiet. Unusual for her, especially now that she and Zeke were out in the open with their relationship, but before I could check on her, I had to make sure there were no immediate threats around us.

My eyes scanned the property as I set the bag I'd been holding on to since Beatrix's house on the steps. The only thing I could see that hadn't been there before was Beatrix's grey hair floating around her and sparks of magic flickering from her body as she walked the property line.

I kept scanning, as did Rachel and Nikki, then I reached for Rachel's arm, giving it a slight squeeze. "What's going on with you?"

"Being at Beatrix's house, seeing Viktor in person, remembering how I almost died just a few days ago? It's a lot to process. I'll be okay, and I'm good to fight. I just need some time to accept our new circumstances."

Here I was just thankful to have them back and alive that I hadn't considered how the experience of being trapped inside a magically burning house would affect them, regardless of if they'd survived.

"I'm sorry, Rachel. I know it's a lot, but I'm here if you want to talk," I said, not really knowing what else I could do to make the trauma easier for her to process.

She gave me a small smile. "Thanks."

I nodded and squeezed her arm one more time before letting go.

As I did another scan of the front side of the property, shouts sounded from the backyard, and I spun around toward the raised voices. "I'll be right back." Then, I disappeared in a blur, flying faster over the yard than ever before.

CHAPTER 13

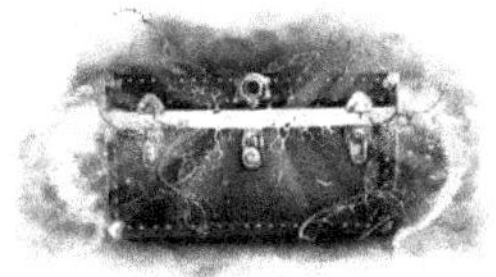

My speed was over the top and made my chest burn with its force as I curved around the house. Though, I didn't have time to decipher what the changes meant, because Maciah had some guy pinned against a tree.

The newcomer's hands were up in surrender. He was wearing dark jeans and a plain white tee, more casual than the vampires I was used to seeing. His hair was longer and dark blond, falling just above his shoulders and pushed back behind his ears.

His eyes were the same mahogany I was used to seeing in Maciah's nest, but I didn't recognize him. I stepped forward with caution as I listened in on their conversation.

"What are you doing here? I'm not going to ask again," Maciah snarled.

"I saw what happened in Portland. I had to make sure she was okay," the guy answered.

"You had no reason to do that. She's my responsibility," Maciah said.

She who? Me? I didn't know this guy, so I wasn't so sure, but Maciah was protective of whoever he was talking about.

"Come on, Mac. You know I had no choice. She was better off, but I couldn't completely walk away."

Mac? That was a new name for Maciah and seemed pretty personal.

"You made a choice, Bennett. Live with it and leave before you cause more harm," Maciah demanded with Zeke and Eddie flanking him.

Oh. Bennett. Nikki. Shit. I hoped they hadn't followed me.

I moved to race back around the house, but I was too late. Nikki and Rachel had turned the corner, and I couldn't stop what was about to happen.

Nikki froze for a moment and gasped, the sound loud enough that Bennett heard her. The pained look on his face told me he still very much cared about my friend, but he was an idiot either way.

I blurred until I was in front of Nikki, holding her arms. "You can walk away and be done with him. Or you can talk to him. This is your decision, and I'll make sure you're supported no matter what you choose."

Nikki had unanswered questions about why Bennett disappeared on her five years ago. She hadn't let him go, and if seeing him now would give her closure or whatever she'd been missing, then she deserved for that to happen. Regardless of what anyone else thought.

Nikki was still staring past me. "I need a minute, but I'd like to talk to him if he's staying."

"Oh, he's staying until you say you want him gone," I replied.

Nikki nodded and disappeared toward the house. I turned to Rachel. "Was that the right thing?"

"Absolutely. Maciah and Zeke won't agree. They watched how hurt Nikki was, and even though Maciah doesn't show emotion very often anymore, I know it pained him when Bennett left, too."

Rachel was right. Maciah hadn't expressed in detail how he'd felt back in the hotel room, but he'd opened up enough about that time of his life, and I was glad to know I'd been right that the vampires had always known Maciah cared, even when he'd had trouble showing it after feeling betrayed one too many times.

"Let's go make sure they don't start throwing punches." Rachel sighed, and I followed after her.

Bennett was still pinned to the oak tree, and Maciah was glancing back at us as we approached. "Where's Nikki?" he asked, looking behind us.

"She went inside, but she does want to talk to him. Just not yet," Rachel answered.

Maciah grunted and gave Bennett another shove before releasing him. "You're lucky she's more forgiving than the rest of us."

"I said I was sorry, Mac. I didn't have another choice." Bennett begged for his understanding.

Maciah sneered at him. "We always have a choice. Sometimes we're just too scared to make the right one."

As the words left Maciah's mouth, I wondered if he was not only talking to Bennett, but to himself. He struggled a lot with his fear, but maybe he was finally learning that fear didn't have to win.

Zeke, Rachel, and Eddie stayed with Bennett, and I left with Maciah, taking his hand as he stormed off.

I let him stew for several minutes as we walked as far away from the others as we could get without leaving the property.

Maciah stared up at the stars, the tension leaving his shoulders a little more with every passing second.

"I know this is a lot for you, but maybe it's a good thing Bennett showed up. We could use the help if you think you can still trust him," I said softly.

"He was my best friend before Zeke. When he left, it changed everything for me. I thought I could trust him to have my back, and he left without a word."

I leaned against his shoulder, trying to offer comfort. "People do things they shouldn't when they're scared. I think you've experienced that more lately than ever before."

He nodded, more of the rage fading away from him. "Still pisses me off."

"I know, and I'm not saying you have to let him back

in, but the longer you hold on to your anger, the more you're hurting yourself."

Maciah glanced down at me, eyes soft and caring. "When did you become so aware of everything?"

"When I became a vampire and all the things around me amplified tenfold. If I hadn't let go of my anger and taken control—just like you taught me—then I wouldn't have been able to fight for what I want most."

"And what's that?" he asked, stroking my cheek with his thumb.

"Peace," I answered without hesitation.

That was something I hadn't truly had since I was fourteen. I'd long forgotten what it felt like to be content, but Maciah and his nest had shown me glimpses, and that was what I wanted most in my life.

I still intended to hunt vampires, which I knew wouldn't always be easy—or peaceful—but with my family's murderers gone and Maciah set free from his past with Silas, I knew we'd find a way to always feel safe and content with our new vampire family.

"Peace sounds nice," Maciah murmured before pressing his lips to mine.

I kissed him once, then pulled back. "Are you going to be okay?"

He nodded. "I won't let Bennett distract me unless Nikki wants him gone. It's up to her now."

"And you're sure that we can trust him? Is there a chance he might have returned because someone sent him to us?" I asked, knowing we couldn't be too careful. It was still likely we had a vampire from the nest out there who'd been working with Dmitri and potentially Viktor.

"We can. I might not like him at the moment, but Bennett is a good vampire. He'd never work with anyone like Viktor."

Maciah seemed positive, and I wanted to believe him, so I let it go. I'd quiz the new vampire myself when the time was right to be sure, though.

"Let's go inside and wait for Beatrix. Looks like she's about halfway around the property," Maciah said.

"I need to check on Nikki, too," I said as we walked toward the house and scanned the area again. Until Beatrix was done, we couldn't be too safe.

Nothing stood out to either of us as we stepped onto the porch and I picked my bag up, surprised nobody else had already grabbed it.

Maciah held the door open for me, and I stepped inside first. Zeke and Eddie were staring at Bennett, and I saw a flash of Jazz's red hair disappear into the hallway.

I turned to Maciah, lifting the potions up. "I'm going to put this in our room and then find Nikki. Please, be nice."

He grunted, but I could also see a grin through his tough act. I knew having Bennett here brought back ill feelings, but there was also a small part of Maciah glad to have his friend back. He might be able to hide that from the rest of them, but not me.

Before I worried any more about what the guys might do, I dropped the bag of potions on our bed, then went in search of Rachel and Nikki, assuming they were in Nikki's room.

Sure enough, when I opened the door, they were both sitting on the bed. I settled in next to them, crossing my legs and having no clue what to say. I was getting better at caring and being there for people, but boy troubles weren't really my thing.

"So, how's it going?" I asked when neither of them said anything.

"Nikki's switching between murderous thoughts and wanting to drag him back to her room after kicking us out," Rachel answered dryly.

"Well, that makes sense. He is pretty hot. The long hair fits with what I've learned about him, but it would also be fun to drag him across hot coal holding only his dark-blond strands," I said.

Nikki finally cracked a smile. "I've pictured nearly that exact scenario, but it was razor blades instead of coal."

"Nice." I gave her a fist bump, glad my humor was helping.

"So, what now? Make him sweat it out downstairs for the rest of the night, or however long you need? Or are you going to rip the band-aid off and see what he came to say?" I asked.

Nikki's fingers fidgeted over her lap. "What would you do?"

"I'd make him stew for at least another hour or two,

then waltz down those stairs, demand his presence, and give him hell privately," I answered.

She nodded, then glanced at Rachel. "What do you think?"

Rachel reached a hand to Nikki. "It's not a bad idea as long as you're ready for what he might say. Have you thought about what you'll do if he wants to come back to the nest? Back to you?"

Nikki shook her head at Rachel's very valid point. It wasn't just about Nikki facing the man who scorned her. She had to think about how that decision might affect her future as well.

"I've missed him, but I don't want him to think that what he did was acceptable if I speak with him or touch him or let him see what he still does to me," Nikki said, a stray tear falling down her cheek.

"Do you believe his actions were meant to be maliciously hurtful toward you?" I asked, and she shook her head. "Do you believe he really loved you?"

"I do," she answered, a smile growing on her face.

Rachel grinned as well. "It was almost sickening being around them before."

"Then, to me, you're only hurting yourself by not speaking your piece and seeing what he has to say. Only then can you decide what to do. You're a smart vampire. You'll be able to ferret out any lies he might try to get past you," I said, hoping that I wasn't helping Bennett further break Nikki's heart by encouraging her to talk with him.

I just knew that if I hadn't gone to Maciah and faced

him as soon as I was able, then I might have run instead, and I didn't want to picture where I'd be without these vampires in my life. Not anymore.

Maybe Bennett could still be Nikki's happily-ever-after, but she was going to have to take a risk I wasn't sure she was ready for.

Kalynne
KALYNNE_ART

CHAPTER 14

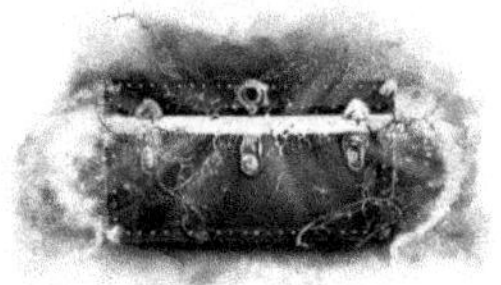

Time was no longer relevant now that I didn't need sleep. Of course, I liked my rest when I could shut off my mind and forget the world for a little while, but there was too much going on to even consider that.

So, as I stretched out on the couch, tossed my legs over Maciah's, and glanced at the clock on the wall, I wasn't really surprised when it showed it was four in the morning. The sun would be coming up in another hour or so, and I'd have to test Beatrix's magic, hoping it worked.

She was nearly finished with the shield around the property. I felt bad that it was taking so long, but I was also glad, because that made me believe she was putting real effort into keeping us safe.

I wasn't sure how to feel about her making an extra effort with me merely because I was some sort of responsibility to an old friend. I didn't want to believe it could be that simple, but then again, I didn't know witches or how their loyalty worked.

Vampires weren't often loyal, and that was all I'd put my focus on for the last seven years. Witches and wolves weren't my problem before, but now that I wasn't human, maybe I'd have to find some time to learn more about all of the other supernaturals.

"Where are the others?" I asked Maciah.

"Jazz, Gabe, and Nick went to their rooms. Eddie is outside somewhere checking on things. Zeke and Rachel… Well, I don't pay attention to them anymore. They're good on their own together. And I think Bennett is sulking somewhere around here while I assume Nikki hides away in her room."

I laughed. "Okay, by 'others', I didn't mean everyone, just the ones who had been in here when I'd gone upstairs, but thanks for the play-by-play."

"You're welcome," he said, pulling me closer to his chest.

The front door opened, and we looked up to find a frazzled Beatrix standing in the doorway. "You need a smaller property."

She kicked the door closed before coming into the living room and throwing herself down onto the chair. "I'm going to sleep for a week, but you guys are safe in here. At least safe enough to have a big head start on anyone trying to break in."

"What does that mean?" I asked.

"Well, if Viktor brings a witch with him, I doubt she's

going to be weak, so I'd expect her to attempt to break through. No shield is unbreakable with the right power going against it, but this one will take work to get through. Though, it's not the same as mine. People can see in and hear you, so you're not completely protected. Something of that magnitude would have taken more time and help."

Maciah sat up, leaning his elbows on his knees. "Thank you, Beatrix. I know you don't like to involve yourself in business like this, but your actions won't be forgotten."

She smirked. "Oh, I know. I won't let them be. Also, only the people inside the shield right at this moment can come and go as they please. If you're ready to take it down, throw this at the barrier." She tossed Maciah a vial of smoky grey liquid, and he tucked it into his front pocket.

"Understood."

Beatrix groaned and got up. "This witch is getting too old for all-nighters." She walked over to me and tugged me up.

As I stood, she placed both of her hands on my cheeks and squeezed until my lips pinched together. "Don't worry about anything. Just do what you've always done, and everything will work out how it's supposed to," she said, then released me and moved to turn away, but I caught her arm.

"What if I'm not okay with how things are 'supposed to' work out?"

She shrugged. "That's life. We don't always get what we want, but that doesn't mean you stop fighting."

Beatrix continued for the door, and we watched her leave. Maciah pulled me back to his lap. This time I was sitting right on top of him.

"Are you worried?" I asked, because we really had no clue what we were going to do next. We had ten vampires inside the shield, and while I knew the original power inside me was now a natural thing I could access without much thought, I wasn't sure that would be enough.

Viktor wasn't stupid. He'd been planning for this, and he was ready. We had no idea what we were getting into.

"Yes and no. Beatrix is right, as you've also been this whole time. We can't let fear rule our decisions. Facing Viktor is something we have to do. If we're meant to survive, then we will. If we're not, then I know I'll find you in another life. Either way, this isn't the end. It's only the beginning for us."

My heart fluttered. Maciah had a way with words when he wanted, and I hoped like hell he was right.

Maciah pressed his lips to mine, and the sound of a piano played softly in the background. A smile spread on Maciah's face.

"What?" I asked.

"Bennett is trying to get Nikki's attention. He used to play for her all the time. That's why that piano is even here."

I listened to the melody change from a heartbreaking tune to one filled with love. He played fluidly, drawing me in with the music, and I wasn't normally even a fan of the piano.

"I told Nikki she should hear him out, so she wouldn't have to wonder what might have been," I said, hoping he'd agree with my choice.

Maciah nodded, leaning his head back against the couch. "Bennett is a good vampire and he loved Nikki. Still does, from the sounds of it. You gave her good advice." Maciah paused and grinned at me. I was glad he could finally see I'd been right before. Then, he added, "Knowing Nikki almost died hit Bennett hard, and I don't think he'll leave her again unless she tells him to."

"Did he tell you any of that?" I asked.

"He didn't have to. I know Bennett. He hasn't changed in the five years since I saw him last. The look in his eyes, the way he softened when he saw Nikki, and the way his shoulders drooped when she ran from him. I know what he wants, but I also know he loves her enough to walk away if that's what she needs."

I'd thought Bennett was a Grade-A asshole before for leaving, but I could see he and Maciah were probably very alike. The way Maciah spoke about Bennett told me everything I needed to know, and I hoped our two friends found a way to work things out and be happy again.

The music stopped. Nikki's voice echoed through the quiet house.

"What are you doing?" she hissed.

"Playing a song," Bennett replied innocently.

A huff I was sure came from Nikki sounded, then silence for a few more beats.

"Would you like me to stop?" Bennett asked, and I could hear the smirk in his voice.

Nikki must have shaken her head because the piano resumed.

I glanced at Maciah. "We should give them some privacy."

"Or better yet, give *us* some privacy." He picked me up, cradling me to his chest and carrying me to our room.

The door clicked closed behind us, and he settled me onto the edge of the bed before running his hands down my legs. "I've been wanting to take this dress off you since I saw you in it earlier."

Luxury was comfortable. I'd almost forgotten I was still wearing the shimmering little black dress.

Maciah pulled one heel off me, then another, kissing my ankles before working his way back up my legs. His fingers slid under the hem of my dress, raising the fabric until it bunched at my waist.

His hand cupped my center. "I don't think I've told you yet, but I like your new clothes."

"You've only seen this one outfit," I said, already breathing heavily in anticipation of the actions to follow.

He hooked a finger around the lacy material, rubbing his finger over my folds. "I've seen enough."

Maciah tugged, and the underwear followed his command, easily sliding down my legs once I leaned back.

Just when I thought he was going to pull the dress over my head, Maciah spread my legs and had his tongue licking at my center before I could blink.

I gasped, sucking in air I didn't need, then moaned loudly as he flicked his tongue across my clit over and over again. Holy hell, I was going to come in a matter of seconds if he kept that up.

His hands gripped my ass, lifting me higher off the bed before his fingers replaced his tongue and I was rocking against his hand, shamelessly needing more of him.

"Please, don't stop," I begged as tingles soared through my body, begging to be released.

Maciah adjusted his hold on me, draping my legs over his shoulders before his tongue lapped at me once again. His thumb kept pressure on my sensitive nub while my hips bucked underneath him, pleading for more.

One of his hands slipped around my backside, applying pressure over my ass. An unfamiliar yet welcome sensation rocked through me, unleashing my orgasm so severely that I nearly blacked out from the overload. As I fought to keep consciousness, my back arched and I cried out Maciah's name, tearing the bed cover from gripping it so roughly while I was locked in the throes of passion.

That had never happened before, but I was here for it.

Maciah gripped my thighs, keeping his mouth over my clit until the tremors in my legs ceased. He kissed each of my inner thighs, then moved up my stomach, lapping at my belly button like it was the last source of water in the Sahara.

My hips jolted from his assault. I didn't think I could take any more after that release, but he was quickly proving me wrong.

He pulled the dress over my head, his eyes heating as he finally got a peek at the matching black lace bra to my underwear. His mouth homed in on my left breast and sucked my nipple between his lips.

I clawed at his shoulders, holding on for dear life as he slowly built me up again. Damn, I would never get enough of this man.

He moved to my other tit as he unhooked the clasp in the back. The bra straps fell down my shoulders, staying there until Maciah had his fill.

His hand gripped my chin possessively while the other one tugged the bra from my arms. "All mine," he murmured against my lips.

"Always," I whispered.

In a blink, he had his pants off and I tore his shirt from his chest. Once he was gloriously naked, he propped my legs over his shoulders again, and he slammed into me with one thrust.

I cried out, calling his name and digging my nails into his forearms as I held on for dear life.

I was already ready to come again, but I was going to wait for him, knowing how much better it was from his previous torture.

He pounded into me, keeping his eyes locked on mine

and stroking my hair out of my face with one hand while the other pinned my shoulder to the mattress.

"I love you," I murmured.

"Love you so damn much," he nearly growled before lifting me a little higher and increasing his pace.

"Jesus," I breathed. There was no more holding my release back. My core tightened as tingles of ecstasy spread up my spine and down my arms.

Maciah tensed and slowed his movements above me, bringing my legs down, so that he could settle himself above me.

"I'll never have enough of you," he said softly.

"Good thing you'll always have all of me."

CHAPTER 15

THE SUN WAS UP, AND THE MOMENT HAD COME FOR ME TO step under its rays for the first time since I was turned. Well, the first time that I wouldn't have to be worried about my skin boiling off.

More than half of our small nest was waiting downstairs to watch, which wasn't really saying much, given there were only ten of us. An unfortunate fact I tried not to think about too much.

"Are you ready?" Rachel asked excitedly.

"I'm not sure if I should be disturbed by your happiness or more comfortable because you have that much faith in Beatrix," I said.

She laughed. "You're overthinking this. A sun protection spell is easy. Any properly trained witch could do it if they felt so inclined. It's just normally they don't want to help."

Yeah, I could understand that. Helping often caused

more trouble than it was worth when it came to dealing with supernaturals.

Nikki blurred into my room, repeating Rachel's previous question. "Are you ready?"

She was glowing this morning, and that made me smile. "Is Bennett waiting out there as well?" I asked with a wink.

"I told you I didn't want to talk about it," she said, trying to be snappy, but there was too much joy radiating off her to make that happen.

I clasped her shoulder. "You don't have to talk for us to know. Vampires, remember?" I pointed to my ears.

She rolled her eyes and snatched my hand from her shoulder. "Come on."

I let her drag me out of the room with Rachel right behind us. As soon as we entered the living room, I saw Maciah talking with Bennett. He didn't seem angry or excited, but more cautious. I understood why, and I hoped that Bennett wasn't going to run off again. I'd hunt him down myself for hurting not only my friend, but my…

I had no idea what to call Maciah. *Boyfriend* seemed too lackluster, but *mate* sounded weird in my head. *Mine* sounded perfect. My Maciah.

Nikki shoved me forward, and the beams of sunshine in front of me loomed closer. The heat from the sun permeated the room, and I ached to swipe my hand through the particles floating in the glow.

Maciah was at my side in the next instant, forcing Nikki and Rachel to back up. "Are you ready?"

I took a deep breath. "You all are making such a big deal out of this, but also downplaying it at the same time. You're confusing the crap out of me."

It wasn't often that I was honest and vulnerable, but I was surrounded by Maciah, Zeke, Rachel, Nikki, and Bennett. Sure, I didn't know Bennett, but I trusted the rest of them with my life. For the first time in much too long, I didn't have to hide who I was. That was priceless to me.

"You'll understand once you step outside, but you can test things out from inside first if you want," Maciah said encouragingly.

I nodded my head and took another step forward. Maciah shadowed my movements.

My hand raised hesitantly, fingers loosening as I brought them closer to the warmth. With my palm up, my skin connected with the sunrays.

My shoulders tensed, but nothing happened. Well, nothing bad.

Heat coated my skin like an old friend as I twisted my wrist around and moved another step closer. There was no burning sensation, but it was different from when I was human. Though, with the tinted window acting as a filter, I couldn't quite place what was different.

Without saying anything, I headed for the front door and slowly turned the handle. It had to already be in the high sixties, and there wasn't a cloud to be seen in the sky.

Maciah reached for my hand, but I stopped him. I wanted to do this on my own, and with one look into his dark eyes, I knew he understood that.

I stepped onto the wooden porch, still covered by the awning, and didn't stop until I was standing on the last step to the yard. The last step before there would be no more cover above me.

A quick glance behind me showed everyone had followed me out, but I didn't let that distract me. I moved onto the sidewalk, fully in the sun for the first time in weeks.

Tingles moved from my head down to my feet. Warmth filled my chest. My head tilted back as I took a deep breath in and out, closing my eyes. Every muscle inside me relaxed as the UV rays soaked into my exposed skin. There was an energy humming through my body that I didn't expect.

A shadow moved in front of me, but he said nothing as I kept my eyes closed. I knew it was Maciah and smirked at the fact that he couldn't stay away for long. I blamed the swirling of emotions rising inside me and not him. With our bond, he was no doubt feeling what I felt, and I hoped it brought him a sense of peace as well.

Minutes later, I opened my eyes to find everyone had moved from the porch and was standing behind Maciah.

Rachel and Nikki were grinning like fools. Zeke was smirking at something only he probably found funny while Bennett was standing there with no expression at all.

But it was Maciah's eyes that held my attention most. They were filled with love and pride and joy.

"I can see why nobody would tell me exactly what to expect," I said.

Maciah closed the distance between us and wrapped his arms around me. I hugged him back, then encouraged him to move to my side since the others were still watching us.

"You can't really describe how the first time feels," Rachel said.

Nikki snorted, and Rachel punched her, hissing, "Not *that* first time."

"Rachel's right. I can still feel the energy from the sun moving through me. Will it always be like this?" I asked.

Zeke nodded, still smiling. "Yep. You'll get used to it after a while."

"What has you so giddy?" I asked.

He shrugged. "This is the first step to starting over. We've been through hell this week, but we've managed to stick together. Like a family."

I'd misread Zeke's grin before. It wasn't mischievous; it was true happiness, something not a lot of us had always known. That was like a pleasant punch to the gut.

"Anything else I should know that I don't already?" I asked.

Bennett hissed as Maciah spun around toward the driveway. I followed their gazes and caught sight of two vehicles speeding down the road that dead-ended at our house.

"Is that Viktor?" Nikki asked.

"I doubt it," Maciah answered.

Well, that didn't matter. Whoever it was, they were coming for us.

"Get the others," Maciah said, and Zeke disappeared in a blur.

The two vehicles skidded to a stop at the end of our driveway. The passenger door to the first one opened and Simon stepped out.

I hissed, taking a clipped stride forward, but Maciah's hand spread across my stomach, stopping my movements.

"Let's see what they do first," he murmured.

"If they can see us, then they can likely hear us," Rachel said.

"They can do both. Beatrix only made a barrier, not an illusion like at her house," I said, thankful she had mentioned that before she left.

Zeke returned with Eddie, Nick, Gabe, and Jazz behind him.

The air around our small group crackled with tension and rage. Some, if not all, of these vampires with Simon were responsible for blowing up our home in Portland. They were responsible for killing three-quarters of our nest. A nest of vampires who only wanted to live a better life and hadn't deserved to be burned alive.

Fury built inside me as the ten of us moved across the yard, heading directly for where Simon stood.

He was still human, something that surprised me even

if he hadn't been able to follow through on getting me to Viktor. Regardless of that, Simon wasn't there with hunters. There were eight bloodsuckers behind him, each one ready for a fight.

Simon's beady eyes met mine, and he smirked. "Hello, Amersyn. Why don't you come out here so we can have a proper chat?"

We weren't outnumbered, but we hadn't been prepared for a fight. I wasn't sure how Maciah wanted to play this. It wasn't something we had talked about, but we should have.

"What do you want, Simon?" I asked instead of addressing the invitation to fight him.

His eyes glowered at me. "You know what I want, and unless you want to be responsible for more deaths, then come out here and make this easy."

I could smell the cigarette stench on his breath even from several feet away and nearly gagged as Maciah stepped forward. "She's not going anywhere with you."

Simon chuckled, looking around Maciah and back at me. "So, you let others speak for you now? Interesting to see how the mighty have fallen."

I snarled at him, blurring right to the opaque shield to face him. "You have no idea what you're talking about."

He smirked. "Don't I, though? Viktor has told me all about you and who your father was and how your family was killed. I always wondered why you were such an uptight bitch, but everything clicked into place when

Viktor told me how he squeezed the life out of your mother."

An inferno of wrath erupted inside me, and I couldn't stop my actions. Simon had no right to talk about my family, to act as if he knew anything about me. He was nothing more than a rat that I was going to squash beneath my boot.

My fingers wrapped around his very human neck and squeezed hard before shoving him against the SUV he'd arrived in. His body made an impression in the back door, and he crumpled to the ground.

Without thinking, I stalked forward, intent on killing him and having no care for the other vampires Simon had arrived with.

Except they had a big interest in me.

Clawed fingers raked down my spine, ruining my shirt and cutting through my hard skin. I whirled around and brought my leg up, kicking the nearest vampire in the gut. He sailed through the air, landing on Beatrix's shield. His arms and legs were pinned against the shimmering barrier, and there was no amount of strength the vampire could use to get free.

He wasn't going to die there, but as the air filled with the smell of burnt skin, I had no doubt he was going to wish he could.

Simon was passed out on the ground, and vampires from both sides were now fighting. I'd started something without asking the others, but we couldn't hide behind the shield forever. Simon might have pissed me off, but he'd also done us a favor.

We needed to show Viktor we weren't afraid of him or the vampires he wanted to send after us.

Another bloodsucker sped toward me. As he leapt from the ground, I ducked and let him fly over me before shoving my fist in the air, connecting with his throat. He tumbled to the gravel, choking and coughing as I stalked toward him.

I didn't have any stakes on me, but that wasn't an issue, not with my new strength and the original power dying to be set free from inside me.

As a second one came for me, I decided to take some aggression out and prolong the fight. I stepped onto the neck of the one I'd just punched, pressing the heel of my boot into his throat, then turned around just in time for the second vampire to catch me before I was ready.

He punched me in the jaw, bones cracked, and I knew if I tried to open my mouth, I'd probably screech in pain. Instead, I ducked, avoiding the second punch while putting more pressure on my foot over the first vampire.

I heard my heel cut through his skin as I let the energy inside me trickle out toward the other vampire. I commanded him to stop with my mind and he froze in place a half-second later. With a smirk, I bent down toward the first bloodsucker and grabbed a handful of his black hair.

"It's a good day to die, don't you think?" I taunted through gritted teeth just before I replaced my boot with my other hand and tore his head from his neck, throwing it toward the shield.

Gruesome, but cathartic.

The second vampire was still frozen behind me as I stood, so I called my power back, giving him a fair fight. I wasn't a murderer. I only killed when it meant keeping myself and innocent people alive.

The one I had a hold of was the last remaining vampire and seemed to know it. He jumped toward me, landing on my back and aiming for my still-not-healed jaw with his fist.

My first thought was to roll forward, throwing him back onto the ground, but after seeing the effectiveness of the shield, I took three steps backward, pressing him into the barrier without hesitation.

His hands grabbed on to my hair as he tried to stay with me instead of being trapped by Beatrix's magic, which was even biting at me while the vampire was still on my back.

I moved to break his hold on me, but Maciah stepped in and forced the vampire the rest of the way back into the shield before shoving me a few feet away.

"Was that fun?" he deadpanned.

I turned around to answer him and saw there were three more vampires on the shield that had joined the two I put there and a few piles of ash around us.

I shrugged, answering Maciah's question. "A little."

My eyes searched for Simon only to find him exactly where I'd last seen him. Blood was dripping from his ears and nose, and I couldn't hear the beat of his heart any longer. I'd killed him with my first and only hit.

Disappointment slapped me in the face. I'd wanted more. I'd wanted to torture him for everything he'd done. For the choices he'd made when he decided to turn on his own kind.

Except I'd forgotten that even though Simon acted like a monster, he wasn't one. He'd still been human. Fragile and weak. Easy to kill.

I'd thought I'd feel at least a small amount of regret if I was ever forced to kill a human, but as I gave Simon's body one more glance, I couldn't be happier for his death.

CHAPTER 16

MACIAH TUGGED ME CLOSER TO HIM, STROKING MY JAW where I'd been punched. I leaned into his gentle touch, wincing at the pain the small gesture caused.

"Are you okay?" Maciah asked.

I nodded, not wanting to speak again so soon. The bones were stitching themselves back together, and I'd be back to normal in no time. Hopefully.

The others joined us, none of them looking hurt or even fazed by the fight.

"That was too quick," Zeke said as he wrapped an arm around Rachel's waist.

Bennett nodded. "I agree. Viktor's men wouldn't have been that easy to defeat."

"If this wasn't Viktor's men, then who were they?" Eddie asked.

"Throwaway vampires. Viktor is the king of using them. It's not a secret, but vampires think if they can manage to survive the situations Viktor convinces them to go into, then that will earn them an honorary spot within his nest. This rarely happens, yet more keep showing up at his doorstep," Maciah answered.

"Still one of the stupidest things I've ever heard," Nikki said, and I nodded in agreement, still not speaking.

"We'll do a perimeter check and make sure this wasn't a distraction," Eddie said, gesturing for Gabe, Jazz, and Nick to join him.

The four of them disappeared, splitting off into groups of two as they circled the property line in a blur.

"What about these ones?" Rachel asked, nodding to the vampires stuck to the barrier.

"We could leave them there as trophies. Might prevent others from trying to get in," Zeke answered with a grin I wanted to match. It was a great idea, and I was absolutely voting for it.

I reached out to offer him a high five, but Maciah pushed my arm back down. "We're not monsters like them. We will kill them. Mostly because if we don't, then they'll only keep trying to kill us, and secondly, we can't leave them here to suffer. They're still people."

Damn him for making sense.

"But the idea was good," Zeke added, and Rachel elbowed him.

I rubbed my fingers over my jawline and sighed when the action didn't hurt. "So, if these were throwaway vampires, does that mean the real ones will be showing up soon?" I asked, because we needed to be more prepared if so.

"It's possible. I need to get a hold of some people and call in some favors before that happens, but we should meet first to discuss a few things," Maciah said.

I hoped his mention of favors meant he was finally going to accept the wolves' offer of help. They'd seemed willing enough when we'd been at Nyx, and I didn't peg them as the kind of people who would renege on something like that.

"I can make some calls, too," Bennett said, and all eyes went to him.

"Where have you been all this time, bro?" Zeke asked.

Bennett grimaced. "I've been around, but I've made some acquaintances. Ones that enjoy death."

"I'm not sure we need that kind of help," Maciah said, and I agreed. That description didn't fit with someone I would consider trustworthy of having our back.

"Just think about it. They're not bad people. Just dangerous," Bennett said.

Hmm, I wasn't sure there was a difference, but then again, I used to think all vampires were the scum of the Earth and I'd been proven wrong, so I'd let Maciah decide how he handled Bennett's offer.

"What about the vehicles and, more importantly, Simon's body?" I asked. He wasn't going to disappear into ash like the rest of them, but I had no desire to bury him, either.

"We'll pull the vehicles inside the garage. We might

need them. And I'll ask Eddie to dig a hole that we can throw Simon in at the back of the property never to be seen again," Maciah replied.

That worked well enough.

"I'll go grab some stakes," Zeke said before disappearing. At least he was going to take care of the vampires that were being electrocuted on the barrier. It was one thing to kill the bloodsucker while they were trying to do the same to me, but now that the adrenaline had worn off and Maciah's speech about not being monsters sunk in, I wasn't sure how I'd do with stabbing them when they were helplessly locked against a magical shield.

Yeah, my conscience was weird like that.

Maciah led me back through the yard and toward the house with Nikki and Bennett right behind us. Rachel must have gone with Zeke, because I didn't see her anywhere.

I almost didn't like all of us having men at our sides. The dynamics had changed, and I wasn't a fan of that type of change, but I knew the mess with Viktor wasn't helping, either.

Even with Silas after us, we'd still had moments of normalcy, but ever since the nest blew up, nothing had been normal.

I wanted that back more than anything. Not just for me, but for all of us. I could feel the layer of stress smothering each of us, even when we were smiling.

We entered the house as Zeke was coming out with four stakes.

"Where's Rachel?" I asked him.

"She stayed inside, getting ready for us to meet," he said, then nodded at Maciah. "I'll move the cars in after I'm done and then be right in."

"Have Eddie take care of that. They should be done with the perimeter check," Maciah answered, then we continued toward the small conference area that I assumed used to be a dining room.

Rachel was already in there. She had glasses of blood at every chair and was moving around the room, straightening things that didn't need straightening.

I went to her and forced her to stop moving. "Hey."

She met my stare with her bright eyes. "Hi."

"Are you good?" I asked.

She nodded. "That was just unexpected. I like to be mentally prepared for fights like that."

"I'm sorry," I said since I was the one who crossed the barrier without talking to any of them first.

She scoffed. "I would have done the same. That hunter had no right to talk to you like that."

I gave her hand a squeeze as my thanks before urging her to sit down. I was afraid she would start dusting things or something.

Nikki took the seat next to Rachel with Bennett right beside Nikki. I moved one down, so Zeke could be close to Rachel, then Maciah sat as well.

I reached for the blood and grinned. It was

peppermint flavored. Normally, that wasn't something I liked, but I knew Rachel had needed the distraction of doing a little extra, so I took a long drink and thanked her for getting everyone sustenance.

"It was nothing," she said with a wave of her hand.

"Even though the calls I need to make are important, there are some things we've been ignoring that can't wait any longer," Maciah said, getting right to the point.

I glanced at the door that was still cracked open. I thought to close it, but there were only ten of us around the property. Privacy probably wasn't necessary.

"Are there any objections to having help from the wolves?" Maciah asked first.

My eyes went to Rachel, wondering if the Sam chick mentioned before would be included in that help and if that would cause Rachel any added stress.

She smiled at me, almost as if she'd read my mind, and I nodded at her before responding to Maciah's question.

"What does it mean to have their help? Will the pack just show up here ready to fight?" I didn't know what to expect since I'd never worked with wolf shifters.

"I'll give Roman a call and see what he can offer. We won't ask for anything other than what they're comfortable with. I trust they'll do whatever they can to assist us, but only if everyone is good working with them again. And yes, I think they'd merely show up ready to fight as we did for them."

"No issues for me to have them here," Nikki said.

"Agreed," Rachel added.

"You know I don't have a problem with it," Zeke said as he waltzed into the room, taking the seat next to Rachel.

Maciah stared at Bennett, and I was a little surprised he was waiting on the vampire's confirmation.

"Is this going to be a problem for you?" Maciah asked him.

Bennett's jaw tensed, telling me there was a story there I probably needed to know, just in case things didn't go as planned.

"I'll be fine."

Maciah nodded. "Good. Now, something we've avoided for too long is the vampire who let Dmitri into our nest when Amersyn was taken."

My chest twisted as I recalled that day. The guards had their faces covered, and I hadn't thought anything of it then. I also hadn't been a vampire at that time, so deciphering someone just by their scent wasn't something I'd been capable of.

"Maybe they died in the explosion," Nikki suggested.

"Maybe, but what if they didn't?" Maciah replied, asking a question none of us wanted to think about.

"Are you implying that you have a rat in your nest of only ten vampires?" Bennett's voice became rough as his hands fisted on the tabletop.

"I'm saying it's a possibility we need to consider," Maciah said evenly. He was acting awfully calm for someone who might have a traitor on his hands. I wouldn't be acting the same, but he'd had decades of leading experience, so I trusted his instincts.

"Then, we need to question everyone here, including those of us in this room," I said.

Rachel gasped at my suggestion. I knew it was hard to fathom, but none of us were immune to persuasion. We all had something to lose, and one well-given threat was all it took to make someone do something they normally wouldn't even dream of.

"We'll do that tomorrow. Let's not tell the others until then," Maciah said casually, and I was getting the feeling he was putting on a show the rest of us didn't have advanced tickets to.

"So, what else? The wolves, a potential traitor? What about Viktor?" Zeke asked.

Maciah leaned back in his seat and snarled. "He's a problem. More of one than I'd like to admit. I think we're safest staying here. We can't win against him in a fight unless we have plenty of help. We can reevaluate once we know who we can count on."

Rage wanted to unleash from me, but I met Maciah's dark eyes, and he nodded at me. He was trying to tell me something, and I didn't know what exactly. He was lucky I trusted him. Otherwise, I'd be beating some sense back into him in front of everyone without a second thought.

"You don't think we can beat him, even with my abilities?" I asked, getting that information out there because it seemed to be the direction Maciah was headed if I was reading things at least partially correctly.

"Don't take this the wrong way, Amersyn, but you're not ready. We don't know how to train you with your original powers. They're useless until you can understand how to wield them properly," he answered, and I glanced around the table to find everyone else was in agreement with him.

That alone made me realize Maciah was putting on a show, because there was no way Rachel and Nikki would have agreed with Maciah otherwise.

Except if those of us in this room had figured out Maciah's scheming, then what was to say whoever this show was for didn't as well. We needed to be more convincing.

CHAPTER 17

I SHOVED BACK FROM THE TABLE AND SLAMMED MY FIST down. "You know what? Screw you, Maciah. You always act like you know me so well and what's best for everyone else. You started this meeting appearing to give us a voice, but you're still trying to control us. I'm not weak. I can handle my abilities."

Energy unfurled from inside me, lashing out at everyone near us and probably anyone in the house, but there was no noticeable intent behind my push of power.

I wanted to prove Maciah right and give the traitor a sense of false hope. If one really was in the house and passing information off to Viktor who already knew I was an heir, then it was best to give them every reason to underestimate us.

On top of that, this pretend spat would make it seem as if the foundations of our group weren't as solid as they once were. That was a weakness Viktor could exploit, making him more confident in getting what he wanted.

Even though we'd tried and failed to use this same tactic against Silas, I was growing more confident by the minute that the outcome wouldn't be the same a second time.

Maciah stood and met my fiery gaze. "You can't even keep me down. What makes you think you can control someone like Viktor?"

"I'll figure it out," I snapped.

He raised a brow. "Will you? Do you really think you can do this on your own? You need to listen to me, Amersyn. I know what I'm talking about, and I can keep you safe."

I called my energy back to me. "Maybe, maybe not. I guess we'll find out."

"If you're not going to work as a team, then we need to know right now," Maciah said as he took his seat again.

I huffed and turned for the window. The vehicles Simon arrived with were gone from the driveway, so all of our vampires should have been back inside the house already. Which hopefully meant that the little show we were putting on wasn't for nothing.

"I'm not going anywhere, but I don't like being talked down to. I can, and will, figure out the power inside me," I said without turning back to face them.

Maciah was behind me in the next second. "I hope you can, because there's nowhere else that I'd rather you be than by my side."

And just like that, we had made up. Well, enough that it wouldn't be suspicious for us to hold a civil conversation or be alone together.

"I need some air," I said, moving out of Maciah's hold and out the door without waiting for a response.

Sure enough, Eddie, Nick, and Jazz were standing in the kitchen, which was the closest room to the one I'd just stormed out of.

"Everything get cleaned up?" I asked them curtly.

All three of them avoided my intense stare, but Eddie finally nodded. "Yes. We put the vehicles in the garage as requested and took care of the hunter."

I moved my gaze over them, suddenly suspicious of everyone even though I'd already known that having a traitor among us was a real possibility. Maciah's show and words were merely a reminder that several things had happened around us that weren't right. Things that should have been bigger red flags than we'd made them out to be previously because too many other things were happening at once.

For one, Viktor finding us so quickly the night before was odd. Dante said he was an excellent tracker, but maybe he'd also had a push in the right direction. Along with knowing exactly when to send the drones in to blow up the nest and Dmitri being able to take me unaware at Viktor's instruction.

Not for the first time, I thought back to that day, trying to recall any identifying details about the guards, but I had nothing.

Before things could get awkward, I left the three vampires in the kitchen and headed outside for the air I'd mentioned I needed.

Eddie seemed trustworthy. He'd been helping with things like Dave and organizing the attack on Silas and never pushed back when he was told to do something. There were no red flags for me about him, but maybe that was exactly why we should be looking at him.

Then, there was Jazz who was hardly ever around and hardly ever spoke to the rest of us. That made him suspicious, but did it make him a traitor?

Nick and Gabe were the ones that I knew the least about, but they were also right there in the middle of skepticism. Around enough, but never really doing anything to stand out. Perfect traits for a spy.

As I exited the house, my frustration only grew more. We didn't have time for traitors, and I wished Maciah would have been able to warn me before throwing the idea out there. Though, I assumed it wasn't something he'd really thought about until just before our impromptu meeting.

I pulled my replacement phone from my back pocket —thankful I'd been able to salvage phone numbers from my cloud backups—and decided to take things into my own hands while I waited for him to find me.

Cait had texted me the night we met at Nyx. It was time I responded.

Me: It's Amersyn. I had to get a new phone. Things haven't gone as we hoped around here. Are you busy?

While I waited for her response, I found myself at the front of the property, standing as close to the barrier as I could get without touching it.

The neighborhood was spread out, and I could only see one house down the street. Far enough away that I hoped they hadn't seen the fight this morning.

Rays of sunlight soaked into my skin, re-energizing me and calming my rapid thoughts. With deep breaths, I focused on the things we did know.

Viktor wanted me dead.

We had a traitor in the house, but not one willing to kill me himself.

I was stronger than I'd ever been.

The latter was something I hadn't really had time to process since leaving Beatrix's house. Between Bennett showing up, followed by Simon, plus my time with Maciah, I hadn't had a moment to myself to just feel.

Now that I had a moment…there were several subtle differences I could feel. Once I took the time to notice, there was no denying the power that I held.

I remembered running faster when I'd gone around to the back of the house the night before. When I'd used my ability against the vampire in the fight, the ease of use was similar to blinking.

Whatever Beatrix had done amplified the power inside me and gave me control like I'd never known before.

I held my hands out in front of me, pushing the original energy to the surface. Tingles pricked at my skin, but instead of biting, they were soothing. My heart rate increased, but I didn't feel panicked. I was calmer.

My muscles coiled, ready for action, needing the release of adrenaline a fight would provide, but it wasn't just my physical body that yearned for release. My mind pulsed with need as well.

I closed my eyes and pushed the power beyond my skin, testing its strength and ability. The energy stretched and moved within the confines of Beatrix's shield, moving mostly behind me where there was nothing blocking it.

I had no idea what I was doing, but I already felt better. Drawing the power back toward me, I decided I needed to find Rachel and Nikki to really practice since Maciah was immune to my abilities as my protector. Plus, given Maciah had just made me sound weak to the potential traitor, it wasn't wise to unleash everything I had as soon as I was alone.

When I turned around, I saw Maciah coming toward me. He didn't seem upset or happy. His lips were flat, and his suit jacket was buttoned, but he was sans tie—my favorite look on him.

I kept my face neutral as well. I wasn't sure if we were supposed to still technically be annoyed with each other.

"I'm sorry about that," he said first, keeping his voice low when he stopped right in front of me.

I raised a brow. "A heads up would have been nice."

He glanced back at the house. "We don't have any privacy here. We have to be careful."

"Then, let's go for a walk without telling anyone," I suggested.

Maciah took another look around, then picked me up and sped off through the shield and toward the forest area beyond the small neighborhood on our right.

"I'd have preferred to run myself," I said, half-jokingly, as he deposited me back on the ground, several miles from the house.

He smirked, cupping his hands around my cheeks. "I know." His lips pressed to mine, and I gripped his suit.

Before we could get off track, I pulled back. "Tell me what triggered that scene in the house."

"The fight with Simon. I've known all along we had a problem, but I thought it had either been taken care of with the fire, or the fight with Silas, or maybe they'd fled on their own. Anything could have been possible depending on how deep they are with Viktor."

"What did I miss in the fight? Nothing stood out to me," I said while taking in the large fir trees and bright blue sky above us.

"There was something forced about the interaction. The vampires seemed ready to die, and that's not a normal trait of someone trying to get in good with Viktor. Then, I got to thinking and once I started, I couldn't stop. We're too close to finishing this to ignore the problem I hoped was already taken care of."

I agreed with him. "Do we set the traitor up? Or do we question the vampires like I mentioned?"

My vote was setting the bastard up, but this was Maciah's nest. His people. I would follow his lead.

"I'm not sure yet. I need to call Roman and a few vampires to see how much help we can get and how quickly. Once I know that, then we can decide what to do. If I think we can get the help we'll need, then we'll begin talking about what to do when support arrives. We can overexaggerate on how many that includes with the hope of making Viktor act sooner than he normally would. In the meantime, we'll need to be careful with what we say and do around anyone outside of that office."

I hated to say it, but someone had to. "What about Bennett? Do you know where he's been since he left your nest?"

"He told me a few things. Enough that I believe he's on our team. He wouldn't turn on us and hurt Nikki like that. Not again," Maciah answered, voice full of confidence.

Then, I remembered what I'd been doing before Maciah showed up. "I already texted Cait."

I pulled out my phone, disappointed she still hadn't responded. "I guess they're busy. She hasn't replied yet."

Maciah had his phone out as well, and I saw him scroll to Roman's name. When he pressed call, it went straight to voicemail.

"Let me try Sam," he said.

"Speak," a woman's snarky voice sounded after the second ring.

"Sam, it's Maciah."

She paused. "What happened? Is Zeke okay?"

"Zeke is fine, but I need to talk with Roman," Maciah answered.

Sam chuckled. "He's going to be busy for the next several days."

"So busy that he can't answer the phone?" Maciah pressed.

"Have you ever seen a female wolf shifter in heat for the first time?" Sam asked with amusement in her voice.

Maciah had no response for that, so I took the phone. "Hi, Sam. This is Amersyn. I met Cait and Roman when they came through Portland."

"Ah, yeah. She told me about you."

When Sam said nothing else, I wasn't sure if that was good or not, but I added, "They offered us help if we needed it and we do. Is there anyone else who might be able to step in while Roman and Cait are otherwise occupied?"

"Hmmm," was all she said at first.

Maciah had recovered from his uncomfortableness. "Zeke is fine now, but he almost died, Sam. There are only ten of us left from my nest and one of them is working against us behind the scenes. I wouldn't have called if we had any other options."

"Shit," she muttered. "Are you in Portland still?"

"No, we're in LA," Maciah said, and I could hear papers moving around in the background.

"I'll be there tomorrow morning. I don't know how

many I can bring with me, but I'll have at least three wolves with me."

Maciah sighed with relief. "That's appreciated, Sam. When you arrive, we might mention more wolves coming than there really are as a setup. If you can go along with the plan, it would be easier for us all."

"Yep. I'll send you our flight details," she said, then hung up.

Maciah tucked his phone away as his shoulders lightly shuddered. "I wouldn't ever want to be a wolf shifter."

I laughed at the fact that he was so clearly traumatized by knowing Roman and Cait were locked up somewhere having the time of their life.

I patted his shoulder and gave him a kiss. "Don't worry. That will be us. Just as soon as Viktor is dead."

CHAPTER 18

THE REST OF THE DAY HAD TURNED INTO AN AWKWARD MESS that extended to the next day. Everyone was too on edge to speak about anything helpful, and the vampires who hadn't been present in our little meeting had made themselves scarce, which made it much harder to figure out who we could and couldn't trust.

"We're headed to pick up Sam," Zeke said as he and Rachel entered the living room where Maciah and I had been hanging out most of the early morning.

"Do you want help?" I asked.

Rachel laughed. "Someone's bored."

"Deathly," I groaned.

"We don't have room for anyone else. Wolf shifters like their space," Zeke said.

Yet, they were coming to stay in a house with a bunch of vampires. Good to know.

Then, something occurred to me that we should have

thought of earlier. "How are they going to get through Beatrix's shield?" I asked.

"I already have that taken care of. We're going to have other guests arriving soon as well," Maciah said.

My eyes glared at him, and I pulled my legs off his lap. "You're getting pretty good at keeping things to yourself lately."

"On that note, we're leaving," Zeke said, tugging Rachel toward the door.

She frowned at me before disappearing outside, then I moved my attention back to Maciah. "Who else is coming?"

"It's a secret," he said with a smirk.

"You know I haven't called you a prick in a while. Have you missed the pet name? Is that why you're being a pain in my side?"

Maciah's hands wrapped around my ribs, and he pulled me against his chest before grabbing his phone to turn on music much louder than it needed to be.

His lips pressed against my ear as he whispered, "We're taking down the shield when the wolves get here. Other vampires are arriving, including the ones Bennett mentioned. Most of them will stay in the forest we were at yesterday and only a few will come here. For the rest of the day, we're going to appear annoyed with each other and unprepared and make mistakes that aren't really mistakes. I want Viktor here tonight."

"I don't like all of these games. Someone is going to trip up," I murmured.

"It will be over tonight. I promise you."

I nodded, hoping he was right. "I need to work on my abilities with someone not immune to them."

When we'd come back, Zeke had already begun questioning everyone in the house. A stupid choice that should have involved me, not only to get the truth out of the vampires faster, but so I could practice. Except Maciah had insisted that I needed to stay out of it.

What was the point of me having the ability to pull the truth from lesser vampires if I didn't get to use it? Apparently, it was more important to let the information we were purposely giving get back to Viktor, than figure out exactly who we couldn't trust.

As frustrated as I'd been, it made sense and would also help confuse Viktor as to what I was actually capable of. Not many, including those in the house, knew I'd inherited all of the mind control traits, but they'd do me no good if I didn't understand which powers to use and when.

"Go find Nikki. I need to chat with Bennett and remind him who's in charge around here anyway," Maciah said after turning the music off, so anyone wanting to listen could hear.

"Perfect. You have fun with your pissing contest. I'll see you later." I moved to get up, but he jerked me back down on top of his lap.

"I love you," he nearly growled against my lips before nipping the lower one.

"Love you, too." I bit him back, drawing the smallest

amount of blood before darting out of his grasp and toward the stairs. Another second longer and we'd have ended up in the bedroom, getting nothing accomplished.

I ran into Jazz at the top of the stairs. "Hey," I said casually.

He forced a smile to his freckled face. "Hi."

I was pretty sure that was the first time he'd ever spoken directly to me, so I tried to keep the conversation going. "Everything good up here?"

He glanced around. "As far as I'm aware. Did you get the answers you guys were looking for yesterday?"

I nodded. "We did."

Jazz's eyes widened slightly. "Well, that's good."

"Very good indeed." I grinned at him and pushed a bit of power out.

"Amersyn," Maciah warned from downstairs.

I grinned once more at Jazz. "Gotta go."

Without waiting for a reply, I headed toward Nikki's room just in time to see Bennett opening the door and tucking his collared shirt into his jeans.

He froze when he saw me, then cleared all emotion from his face before brushing past me. He and Maciah were entirely too much alike.

Nikki was laying on her bed, hair in a messy bun and wearing only an oversized shirt. "Good morning," she said.

"Yeah, I can see that," I replied with a chuckle, then added, "I'm going to stay away from the bed and sit right over here."

There was a small table and two chairs that would work just fine for me.

Nikki grimaced. "That's probably no safer than sitting on the bed."

"Savages," I muttered jokingly before throwing a towel over the chair and sitting anyway.

"What's going on?" she asked, getting out of bed and reaching for some pants.

Instead of answering her, I mentally commanded one of my best friends to spin in a circle while patting her head and rubbing circles over her stomach.

It was as hilarious as it was effortless.

"What the hell, Am?" she screeched, tripping over the pants she hadn't quite pulled up all the way and ending up in a tangled mess on the floor. Though, the command hadn't ceased once she was on the ground. When I walked over to help her, she was rolling in circles and still attempting the arm movements.

"Make it stop," she groaned.

I smirked. "Just another minute."

Next, I kept the first command going while also pressing for her to feel certain emotions.

Nikki was giggling uncontrollably one second, then her fangs appeared when I made her hungry, followed by a blank face when I wanted her to feel nothing.

"How?" she deadpanned.

I knelt down and pulled the energy back toward me. "Beatrix. She was able to merge the power I inherited with me. Before that, the only way I was keeping a tight hold on the magic was to keep it locked in a metaphorical box, but that also made using the power much harder."

"I knew she'd done something, but damn girl. There was literally nothing I could do to fight back. I'm curious how Bennett would do if you tried something on him," she said as I helped her up.

Yeah, so was I, considering how well that worked on her.

"So, you can make me do and feel whatever you want. What else?" she asked as she finished getting dressed.

"Tell me, how many surfaces in this room did you christen last night?" I asked.

Nikki's eyes roamed the room. "Six not including the bathroom." Then, she glared at me. "Okay, and you can make people answer you with the truth. Though, I would have told you anyway, so that was sort of cheating."

I grinned and retook my seat at the small table. "I know you would have, which is why I asked. I'd never make you tell me something you normally wouldn't feel comfortable with."

She sat across from me. "You're getting soft. I like it. I mean, I liked the you when you arrived, but now you're like a mix of me and Rachel. Which is more fun, because I'm never certain of what you'll do, like when Maciah was being a jerk in the meeting yesterday."

I nodded, not really wanting to talk about that in the house. "Well, at least we're moving past that. Mostly."

"Did Rachel and Zeke leave to go pick up Sam and the wolves yet?" Nikki asked.

"Yeah, right before I came in here, but I don't want to talk about them." I leaned back in my chair and grinned. "I take it things are going well between you and Bennett? Possibly even picking up right where they left off?"

Nikki took the seat across from me, grinning like a fool. "Yes and no. I threatened him with castration if he ever attempted to 'protect me' again by leaving, then proceeded to list off all the ways I'd learned to kill someone since we last saw each other. Only when I had him inching for the door did I let him know we could start over."

I shook my head, chuckling. "And by starting over, you mean you finished making up by having wild sex all over your room?"

She shrugged. "That's how we started out the first time. Why not the second as well? It was an instant attraction when I met him all those years ago. As soon as I had pushed the guilt of wanting someone other than the husband who thought I was dead out of my mind, I made sure Bennett knew I wanted him back then."

There was a happiness in her voice I hadn't heard before. Nikki deserved that, and I was glad she'd talked to Bennett instead of pushing him away.

"Want to go beat the hell out of each other outside?" I asked. There wasn't much that we could talk about truthfully inside the house anymore. At least not until after tonight if all went as Maciah had planned.

"Abso-freakin-lutely," Nikki replied, just as I knew she would.

CHAPTER 19

Poor Nikki. I really did love her, but she no longer believed me when I said it.

We ended up outside in the front yard as planned, but instead of fighting fair, I used my now-easily-accessible abilities to make sure she didn't stand a chance against me, like making her think her legs were noodles when she tried to kick me or that there were spiders crawling all over her when she was running.

"You're kicked out of the womance," Nikki huffed as she wiped grass from her leggings.

"You can't do that. Once I'm in, there's no removing me until I'm dead," I joked.

She sneered at me. "Maybe that can be arranged."

I walked toward her, throwing an arm around her shoulders. "Oh, come on. We're just having fun."

Nikki's elbow crunched at least two of my ribs. "*Now* we're both having fun."

I winced, backing away and ready to go again, but the front door opened just as the Range Rover stopped at the end of the driveway.

Maciah gestured for us to follow him and all joking around ended. He had the vial from Beatrix that would take down our only protection. I knew what he was hoping for, but I was worried about things backfiring on us. There was a possibility that we were preparing for something bigger than we could handle.

Regardless, we raced ahead to the property line, and I glanced up at Maciah. "Are you sure about this?"

He uncorked the bottle. "Positive. If we want to keep control, this is the only way."

Nikki and I watched as Maciah threw the potion at the shield. There was a puff of smoke where the glass shattered against the magical surface, and we each took a few steps backward. Then, the opaque shield shimmered brighter prior to bursting into tiny sparks of nothing that disappeared before they even hit the ground.

"Looks like one of you bloodsuckers when you die," a female I presumed to be Sam said as she walked toward us.

She was petite, but there were defined muscles lining her exposed arms and legs. Her white-blonde hair was cut short, falling just past her ears, and she had piercing bright-blue eyes that focused on each of us once she stepped past where the barrier had been.

"I'm Sam." She held her hand out to me.

I took it, unsurprised when she squeezed harder than necessary. "Thanks for joining us, Sam. I'm Amersyn."

Her eyes roamed over me before she nodded, then addressed Maciah. "There will be another twenty between our pack and the one we've partnered with that will show up tomorrow. They're driving over while we get things set up for them here." She nodded toward the tree line. "Are we good out there?"

Maciah nodded. "Absolutely. Do you need anything? You mentioned they'd have their own tents, right? Regardless, our house is open to you any time of the day or night."

"We won't need anything from your nest, but the offer is appreciated. The arriving wolves will have everything we need to stay for as long as you need us," Sam said, losing some of the attitude she had arrived with.

Zeke and Rachel had gone up to park the vehicle with the other shifters still in the car, but they were headed our way now and—mother eff—wolves were big.

There were three men with Rachel and Zeke. Each of them was over six feet tall with wide shoulders, dressed in dark clothing. They were certainly going to be helpful, as long as their wolves were stronger than the vampires we'd be facing.

Sam pointed to each of the men as they approached. "That's Collin, Paul, and Rich." They each waved as their names were called. "We're staying in the forest out there," Sam said to them, and they nodded before backing up and…

Mother effer. They shifted right next to us.

I'd been in the know about shifters since shortly after I learned vampires were real, but I'd never actually seen one change from human to beast. Seeing them in action had my pulse quickening.

Their bodies vibrated with tangible energy, then in the next second, they were on four legs without a shred of clothing to be seen.

"Cool, isn't it?" Nikki asked.

I shrugged, not wanting to seem like a fangirl. "Sure."

Two black wolves and one brown one headed toward the forest, running casually as if a human potentially seeing them wasn't a concern.

"Care to come in?" Maciah asked Sam.

Rachel nodded eagerly. "Yes, please do. We'd love to visit longer."

Well, at least Rachel wasn't jealous of the she-wolf any longer. That was going to make things a lot easier.

"I really should be with my pack. I'll let you know when the rest arrive," Sam said, then turned to shift. Her wolf was tan with darker brown paws and was ridiculously quick as she charged after the others.

"I wouldn't mind going on a run. We've been cooped up for days. Anyone else up for it?" I asked, hoping to get the last of the details from Maciah about what to expect moving forward.

"Now is probably the best time," Maciah answered, glancing back at the house.

"I'm going to find Bennett, but you guys have fun," Nikki said, then disappeared toward the porch.

"You guys in?" I asked Rachel and Zeke.

Rachel nodded. "Always."

We took off opposite from the forest, so the wolves could settle in. They weren't putting off vibes of being super comfortable around us with how quickly they'd headed toward the trees, but that didn't bother me. They'd shown up, and that was most important.

Another minute or so later, we were several miles away from the house and standing at the edge of a park already filled with children and parents for the morning.

"Maybe not the best spot," I said, looking around.

"We won't be here long," Maciah said, pulling me to his side.

The moment his arm wrapped around me, my insides softened and I leaned into him, fitting perfectly against his side.

"So, are there any other surprises, or do you have a solid plan in place?" I asked.

"We're going to talk about people arriving to help tomorrow and throughout the week. I believe if Viktor thinks we're gathering an army, then he will act quickly, as in tonight, to avoid dealing with the pack of wolves Nikki will now go mention to Bennett inside the house. In return, Bennett will then tell her that his help is a day behind and won't be arriving when we expected, but that instead of only a few vampires, we can expect a couple dozen showing up in just another day or two."

"I like this plan. If we can get him to come here, then we'll have the upper hand," I said.

"It's not if but when. Viktor will come to us. It's just a gamble hoping he does so tonight," Zeke said.

"Any idea who might be relaying information to him yet?" Rachel asked.

Maciah glowered. "No, but once Viktor is dealt with, if the answer still isn't clear, then Amersyn can force the truth out of whoever is responsible."

I grinned, liking that idea, but also finally seeing the true value in having not done so yet. Maciah had been coming up with ideas as things changed, and he'd made a solid plan, one I was ready to see come to fruition.

"So, we just go back to the house and talk about all the help we're going to have and hope for the best? What if Viktor has too many vampires with him and the four wolves waiting to help aren't enough?" Rachel asked next.

"The vampires Bennett is telling Nikki about, hopefully right now, are already on their way. They'll stay in the forest until Bennett calls for them. The wolves are already aware that they'll have company, but both groups know to give each other space," Maciah answered.

"I feel good about this. Even if they don't show up tonight, we're still going to be ready for them," I said.

"How did practicing with Nikki go?" Maciah asked me.

"Really well. I was able to do several controls at once with little effort."

"Try it on me again," Zeke suggested, likely because he'd been the only one to really break through my ability before.

My eyes met his and I smirked, waiting for the reaction I was hoping for.

Several tears slipped down his cheeks, and he looked at Rachel. "I'm so sorry."

Her eyes widened. "For what?"

"I have no idea," he mumbled through the tears.

Maciah tugged on my arm. "That's probably enough now."

"Is it, though?" I joked as I pulled the power back.

Zeke straightened and hissed at me. "I thought we were friends."

"I thought you might be stronger than my mind control."

Rachel covered her mouth, trying and failing to stifle her laughter.

"Maybe we should head back now," Maciah suggested.

"You don't want to test these superpowers out more than once?" I asked with a smirk.

He shook his head and grabbed my hand. "No, I think we're good here. We'll be ready for Viktor. Hopefully tonight. We have Beatrix's potions. Amersyn has full control over her abilities. We have help that nobody else knows about."

"We're going to beat him," Zeke said, nodding at everything Maciah said.

More than anything else in the world, I hoped they were right. I had all the faith, but I wasn't stupid. Anything could happen, and Viktor had been waiting for this moment a lot longer than us.

He wasn't going to go down easily, but neither was I.

CHAPTER 20

We got back to the house to find Nikki on the couch with Bennett. I hadn't really been able to talk to him, and that didn't sit well with me, especially knowing that Nikki had fully forgiven him.

I went to the kitchen and grabbed a few bottles of blood, setting the extras on the coffee table, then perched on the arm of the couch next to him. "So, Bennett. Tell me about yourself?" I asked casually.

Maciah cleared his throat, pulling me from my spot and toward another chair. "This isn't necessary."

"Maybe not to you. You're welcome to go do whatever it is you do when you're not doing me while I do what I want."

Nikki choked on the blood she was drinking. "Warn a girl before you say something like that next time."

I shrugged and grinned as Maciah sighed, taking a seat and directing me to sit with him.

Rachel and Zeke joined us. "What did I miss?" Rachel asked.

"Just Amersyn talking about all the sex she has with Maciah," Nikki answered.

"Oh. We already know about that. Carry on," Rachel replied, earning me a glare from Maciah.

I rolled my eyes at him. "It's not like I kiss and tell. They can *hear* us." Then, I gave a pointed stare at the rest of them. "Just like we can hear them."

Rachel's hands shot up, covering her face as she buried herself into Zeke's chest. He merely grinned proudly while Nikki laughed and Bennett remained a statue.

Meanwhile, Maciah sighed at my antics, but he said nothing more, because I was right and he knew it. Plus, I was no longer embarrassed talking about our relationship. Accepting there was little to no privacy in this world had been a lot easier once I became a vampire and realized it was also easy to tune out the sounds you really didn't want to hear. Like your friends having sex.

"As I was wondering, who are you, Bennett?" I asked him again since he'd remained quiet throughout the whole interaction.

He had that whole passive vibe going with a heavy dose of I-will-kill-you-without-thinking-twice look in his shadowy maroon eyes. The long, dirty blond hair added to his appeal, and I understood why Nikki had fallen for him in the first place.

"I'm a vampire," he answered nonchalantly.

I gasped, then deadpanned, "Really? I had no clue."

He smirked at me, the first bit of emotion I'd seen on him besides when he was looking at Nikki. "Where did you find this one?" Bennett asked Maciah.

"In an alley, killing vampires," Maciah answered.

Zeke grunted. "She even stabbed me that night."

Bennett raised a brow. "And you still brought her into the nest?"

I snapped my fingers. "Hey. This isn't about me. This is about you. The guy who disappeared for five years and shows up out of nowhere."

Bennett's eyes narrowed and jaw tightened. Good. I'd struck a nerve. That was my intention. I may have wanted Nikki to forgive him for her own happiness, but this guy had also hurt my Maciah. I wasn't going to let him off the hook so easily. Bennett just needed to be thankful I wasn't using my ability to force what I wanted to know out of him. That was a line I was pretty sure Maciah and Nikki wouldn't let me cross.

"You don't know what you're talking about," he said quietly.

I leaned forward, giving Bennett my full attention and making sure I had his, because I only wanted to say this once. "You're right. I don't know, but what I do know is that I'm here now and I care about the people in this room. If you attempt to leave again, I will hunt you down. You won't hurt them again."

Bennett let emotions slip from him, lowering his

guard for the first time. Regret, grief, and hope were the three most prominent as our gazes remained locked.

"I have no intention of parting from this nest again," Bennett said evenly, truth bleeding from his words.

"Good to know," I said, drawing back and leaning against Maciah before deciding to add one final threat for good measure. "I'd help Nikki turn you to ash if you do."

He nodded and grabbed Nikki's hand. "I won't give her a reason to ask that of you."

I crossed my arms and smirked. "She won't have to ask."

Nikki grinned at me, but pressed closer to Bennett, whispering something to him as Maciah's lips pressed to my ear. "That wasn't necessary, but thank you for caring."

His tone was low and only meant for me, but I shrugged him off, not wanting to make a big deal about the conversation as long as my point was made and understood.

"Now, when are these friends of yours showing up? Tonight, tomorrow, next week?" I asked Bennett next, wanting to get more of our show going now that I'd said my piece with him.

"They'll be here tomorrow, and like the wolves, they'll stay as long as needed," Bennett answered.

"The wolves are on track as well. They might even be bringing in another pack we didn't count on, which will be nice," Zeke said.

"We just need to keep a rotation of people watching the roads for incoming threats. Eddie is outside now, but we should probably have a few of us out there at a time," Maciah added.

I stood up and held my hand to him. "Why don't we join Eddie, then?"

"Not a bad idea." Maciah looked to Zeke. "Figure out a new schedule that will include our guests," Maciah said to him, which I took to mean: "Keep talking about all the help we're not actually going to have so that our message is heard."

Zeke nodded. "You got it."

"Have fun!" Rachel called out as we headed toward the door.

I turned back around to find her snuggled with Zeke while Nikki and Bennett were still speaking softly only to each other. All of them were happy, and I hated that—possibly in a matter of hours—all of what they'd fought so hard for could be taken away.

We had to make sure that didn't happen. No matter the cost.

Our watch with Eddie went on for five hours. We not only stayed on the property, but we also checked on the wolves in the forest and then the streets beyond the house to make sure vampires weren't camping out close by.

Eddie was his normal helpful self, never asking questions, only doing what he was asked to do.

Regardless, Maciah and I kept up conversations about what was discussed in the house as well.

Knowing I was fully capable of getting the truth, yet hadn't, made my skin crawl in anticipation. If Viktor didn't act tonight, then I was going to ask Maciah to reconsider letting me get the information.

We weren't going to be prepared for Viktor if he had too much time to plan his fight against us. Everyone who was coming to help was already there, and we needed this to be done with, no matter how things ended.

"I sent Eddie into the house to get Jazz, Nick, and Gabe for the next watch," Maciah said to me as he reappeared from doing another run around the property.

"You don't want a pair of us with them?" I asked.

"I thought about that, but let's see what happens," he said.

Something about that didn't sit right with me. "Are you sure?"

Maciah glanced around, checking to see if we were still alone at the end of the driveway. "What are you thinking?"

"That we've built up this big plan in hopes that Viktor heads our way tonight. We don't know who to trust outside the six of us. Leaving someone who could be working against us with our vampires who don't know any better might just get more of our nest killed."

Whoever the traitor was, they could start trying to lessen our nest whenever they wanted, and leaving four potential suspects alone didn't bode well for our situation. We could easily end up three vampires less right before being attacked without notice.

Maciah mulled over my words and nodded. "I'll send Nikki and Bennett with Jazz and Gabe. Eddie volunteered to keep watch, so there will be five of them, which is good since it will be dark out soon."

"Thank you," I said, grateful he took my concerns seriously instead of believing he knew what was best.

We headed inside, and Maciah went to find Nikki and Bennett while I chose to go to our room. I was dressed in jeans and a black tank top with boots. Technically, I didn't need anything else, but my back felt naked and that was something I wanted to rectify.

I went into the closet and pulled out my crossbow. I hadn't used it since the fight with Silas, but I decided this wasn't the time to be without my favorite weapon.

Sliding the bow over my back, I reached lower into the bag with stakes and found my leg straps. They secured around both of my thighs, and I filled the slots with eight stakes before adding a few more to each of my boots.

My crossbow was already holding four stake-arrows. Between those and the rest, I hoped I had more than enough.

Maciah came back into the room and grinned at me while holding up the bag Beatrix gave us. "I see we were thinking the same thing," he said.

"Unsurprising." I walked toward him and grabbed the bag we'd been keeping in the safe. My outfit didn't have loose pockets. I considered changing, but Maciah picked up two of the bottles, tucking one into each side of my bra.

"Those should hold just fine there. Just don't let anyone punch you and break them," he said, then started pulling them back out. "On second thought, maybe you shouldn't carry any."

I snatched them back. "I'll be fine. I probably won't even need them."

The abilities I'd inherited from my father and his brothers were fueling my confidence. So long as Viktor didn't show up with a hundred well-trained vampires, the only thing I was concerned with was how soon the fight was going to start.

Viktor had made it clear when he found us at Beatrix's house that he wanted me as his prize—sick bastard. I just didn't know if I was a prize to be kept or murdered. If we lost, my vote was for the latter, but if the dark magic he was mixed up with wasn't immune to my mind control, then there wasn't a chance in hell of us losing.

Maciah's hands brushed over my arms. "I hate seeing you like this."

"It's better than seeing me turn to ash," I countered, making him wince.

"You know what I mean."

I did, but I had no desire to get mushy with him before this fight. That wasn't how we did things, and I wasn't changing that today. We could have all of the "I love you" moments after we'd won.

And if that didn't happen, I had no regrets. I knew how Maciah felt and trusted he knew the same of me.

We didn't need words or moments of validation for our feelings. Our actions, standing by each other's sides, and fighting for the same thing were what mattered most.

Everything else was just white noise.

CHAPTER 21

MIDNIGHT WAS ALMOST UPON US, AND THE LONGER WE HAD to pretend we weren't hoping for a fight that night, the harder it became.

Bennett's vampire friends were in place. Sam and her wolves were ready. The rest of us were equally prepared for Viktor's arrival.

Maciah and I were back on guard duty, but instead of having one or two of the potential traitors with us, we had Rachel and Zeke, so that the others didn't stumble upon all of our new guests.

The four of us headed into the forest only to have Sam meet us at the tree line, and she wasn't alone. There was an older gentleman with her, putting off all the alpha vibes.

He had fine wrinkles at the side of his eyes with short dark-auburn hair and light-green eyes. His shoulders were broad with defined muscles made apparent by his form-fitting black t-shirt. Basically, for an older dude, he was hot.

"Maciah." The alpha nodded curtly.

"Holden." Maciah was just as terse as the shifter.

"Wolf courtesy. I couldn't be in Holden's territory without letting him know. Roman would have thrown a fit and I don't have the patience for that," Sam added dryly.

"It's not a problem for me," Maciah said, then glanced back at Holden. "Are you here to check in, or to help?"

"Maybe both. I haven't decided yet," the alpha answered.

I could sense another dozen shifters in the trees and picked up on several sets of piercing eyes staring at us from the shadows.

"Well, as long as you're not here to be in our way, then you're welcome to do whatever you feel is necessary," I said, hoping to move past the brashness of Maciah and Holden.

Alpha men. Pains in the ass.

Sam smirked. "Cait was right about you."

"Good to know," I replied with my own grin.

Maciah's phone dinged with a message, and the air around him chilled instantly. "Viktor's on his way."

"How do you know?" I asked.

"Zeke and Rachel. They went a mile out. They're racing back from another direction."

"Now is your time to decide what you're doing, Alpha." Then, I nodded at Sam. "Be safe," I said before grabbing Maciah's hand and blurring back toward our house. We didn't have time to see what Holden's answer was. He and his wolves would either be around or they wouldn't be. Simple as that.

Bennett and Nikki met us out front. "There's no sign of Jazz and Eddie, but Gabe and Nick are down the street setting traps for the incoming vehicles," Bennett said.

"How many vehicles?" I asked.

"At least seven." As he answered me, an explosion sounded from down the street. "Maybe less now, but that doesn't mean less vampires."

I pulled my crossbow over my head and double-checked my stakes were ready.

"Too bad you don't have another one of those. We could pick them off from a distance," Nikki said.

"That's exactly why I've always used this baby," I replied, holding it at my side and patting both sides of my chest. The two potions from Beatrix's were still there: stun and bomb. I planned to use the first one on Viktor before attempting to screw with his head. If that didn't work, then I'd try to blow him up before sending an arrow through his chest.

Those were the best scenarios I could come up with inside my head. The likelihood of them happening were...slim to none.

Headlights appeared down the road, but that wasn't all. Vampires, and not our own, were racing toward us. Our time of waiting was up.

Bennett whistled, the sound sharp and high-pitched,

then added, "All of the vampires that came to help are wearing dark-blue shirts. Try not to kill any of them."

The consistent shirt color was a great idea, because I wasn't going to be asking questions before using my crossbow, which I was going to do immediately.

I tucked the stock into my shoulder and took a deep breath as I aimed for the incoming vampires. They were still a good distance out, but I could make a shot from over one-hundred yards with my bow.

Another breath out and I pulled the trigger once, re-aimed and pulled again. The first target went down, but I missed the second and zeroed in on targets three and four. Both of them went down with ease before I pulled my crossbow down and reloaded more stakes.

"What do we want to do about Eddie and Jazz?" I asked when I finished my task. As much as I assumed we should kill them the moment we saw them, I wasn't their nest leader. This was Maciah's call.

"Depends on if they're trying to kill us. Do whatever you have to do," Maciah answered gruffly.

Five vehicles stopped just fifty yards from where we stood, making me think the first small wave of vampires had been from the SUVs that had blown up. Viktor was the first to get out, and his red eyes landed on me immediately.

A smile grew on his face. "Ah, Amersyn. We finally meet." He wasn't near me, but my ears picked up on his words with no problem.

I held my crossbow up and pulled the trigger again.

He was five feet to the left by the time my stake pierced the car door.

"That was uncalled for." Viktor lowered his gaze at me, then snapped his fingers.

Within seconds, there were thirty more of his vampires on the street. Not ideal, but less than there could have been. From the east, Bennett's friends began to appear, and in the distance, wolves howled. We weren't going to be as outnumbered as I originally worried about.

An odd look passed over Viktor's face, but it was gone before I could decipher it, and so was he.

"Where did he go?" Zeke snarled, holding Rachel closer to him.

"Not something we can worry about at the moment," Maciah said, then gave my hand a tight squeeze. "Let's finish this."

I nodded, and we raced toward the horde of vampires headed our way. This was it. There was no more waiting. Our plan had worked, and it was time for us to end the nightmare we'd been forced into.

Rachel threw one of Beatrix's vials at the first row of vampires, and I sent a wave of my mind control out. I'd never tried to control so many of them, and had no idea what was going to happen, but I went for it anyway.

Smoke covered six of them, stunning them just as it was supposed to, and I forced them to sleep. The opposing vampires dropped to the ground in the next second, but another group jumped right over them with guns in their hands.

"Spread out!" Maciah shouted.

I went with him to the right, but we weren't quick enough. A bullet landed in my thigh, burning my muscles. "What the hell is that?" I screeched, trying to dig the slug out while running to avoid being hit again.

Maciah snarled and reached back to pick me up. "The same bullets that Silas's vampires used against us."

With Maciah holding me, I got the bullet out of my thigh and there was instant relief as my body began to heal itself.

Maciah slowed enough that I hopped out of his arms and was running beside him a minute later. We circled around behind Viktor's vampires, still not seeing where he went. A few of them caught sight of us and sped in our direction.

I urged my power to knock them out before they could get too close, but as I sensed the vampire's minds, a dark layer mixed with my own energy.

My mind recoiled from the thick, drowning magic. I had no idea what it was, but I had a feeling it was Viktor interfering with my abilities using the dark magic that Dante had mentioned to us.

Good thing for me, I didn't intend to rely solely on those powers.

Maciah and I leapt into the air at the same time and met the opposing vampires in the middle. I'd already grabbed a stake and struck one before my feet were back on the ground. I kicked his deteriorating body away and snatched another weapon from my thigh as I ducked and twisted out of a vampire's reach.

A head rolled in my path before turning into a puff of ash and I smirked. Maciah enjoyed ripping bloodsucker heads off more than the normal person. That maybe should have bothered me at least a little, but it didn't in the slightest.

Two vampires collided with me, one on each side, but I only had one stake in my hand. I stabbed one, missing his heart and sinking the tip into his ribs while my fist gripped the second one's chest.

The dark energy I'd felt previously wasn't present, and I quickly flattened my palm, sending a wave of magic into him. His red eyes glazed over just before his legs gave out.

I didn't have time to see what happened next as I caught sight of my own stake coming at me. The other vampire had ripped the weapon from his side, attempting to kill me with it. Not that I'd actually die, given I was an original heir, but I didn't imagine I'd heal as quickly as normal if metal penetrated my heart.

Maciah was there in the next instance, his hand slamming into the vampire's arm, then shoving him back a dozen or so feet before the stake could get anywhere near me.

I quickly brought my crossbow up and had a stake aimed for the vampire within the next second, but he was smart and took off in a blur to our left.

"You good?" Maciah asked.

I nodded. "Let's go."

We continued on to see the wolves had arrived. They joined in with the blue-shirt vampires that Bennett invited, and the fight was relatively even. That was a relief I hadn't been expecting so early in the fight, but I knew that could change in the next moment. Especially as I caught a flash of red hair on our right.

"Jazz," I sneered.

Maciah saw him, too, and we took off to track the vampire down. Except when we got closer, it wasn't Jazz running on his own. Eddie was forcefully pulling him along.

Maciah's steps faltered for the briefest of seconds. "Eddie?"

Even though we'd known any of the other vampires could be the one giving Viktor information about us, Eddie had been the one least suspected. He'd always acted loyal, but maybe that should have been the reason we looked closest at him.

Though, it was too late to think about that.

As Maciah's speed got faster, mine began to slow. I reached a hand out to grab him, but my arm felt like lead, and I could barely lift any part of my body as I began lowering to the ground without meaning to.

Eddie stopped then, holding a wide-eyed Jazz in front of him as a shield. "Come any closer and you'll lose another member of your nest," Eddie sneered.

Maciah finally realized I wasn't moving on my own and he blurred back to me, ignoring Eddie's threat.

"I knew you were too weak to lead our nest to greatness when you let a hunter into our home. You could kill me right now, but you'll always choose her. So, instead of being on the losing team, I made my own choice," Eddie said, squeezing tighter around Jazz's neck.

"Get him before he disappears," I demanded to Maciah.

"I'm not leaving you here. I don't care what he does."

Sam's tan wolf came speeding toward us. "I'm not alone. Now, go," I insisted.

Maciah was once again torn, but before he had to decide, Bennett and Nikki appeared.

"I've got him," Bennett snarled.

"So pathetic," Eddie snarled, but Maciah wasn't paying him any attention, which seemed to further irritate the traitorous vampire. Eddie shook Jazz in the air as Jazz did his best to loosen Eddie's grip on him.

Once Maciah had me in his grasp, he finally turned to Eddie. "You haven't been paying attention to what I've been trying to do inside our nest if you think I'm pathetic."

Eddie squeezed Jazz's neck tighter until the vampire's eyes bulged. "You can't fool me anymore, Maciah." With those last words, Eddie twisted, and the snap of Jazz's bones echoed around us as he was tossed to the ground.

Bennett was gone in a blink, following Eddie deeper into the forest. Nikki was right behind them, circling wider and hoping to cut off Eddie from wherever he was running to.

"Are you okay?" Maciah asked me.

My body felt weighed down, but I was fighting back. "I just need another minute. Go check on Jazz."

"A broken neck thankfully won't kill him. Jazz should be okay within the half-hour once he's healed on his own," Maciah said, holding me up, then looked down at Sam's wolf. "Are your wolves good?"

She nodded and either snarled or grinned. It was hard to tell.

"We need to find Viktor," Maciah said to her, and she closed her eyes, inhaling deeply.

I pointed to the tree line. "There's Eddie."

He and Bennett were playing cat and mouse between the shadows, but I had a clear shot of them both. "Let me go," I said to Maciah, focusing my own power on keeping me upright.

He did as I asked, and I grabbed my crossbow with shaking hands. I wasn't sure my aim would be true, but I badly wanted one less traitorous vampire in this fight.

I brought the bow up to my shoulder and took a deep breath. Maciah stood behind me with his hands loosely holding my waist.

Eddie was keeping a steady pace, and I timed his movements as he seemed to be darting between every third tree.

As soon as Eddie disappeared into the shadows again, I pulled the trigger, anticipating where he'd reappear. Sure enough, my stake pierced him, but not in the chest.

The arrow struck his arm, pinning it to his side and throwing Eddie off balance.

Bennett took the opportunity to leap onto Eddie's back. Nikki came racing around the corner just in time for all of us to watch Bennett dig his fingers into Eddie's neck. It seemed as if Bennett leaned in and whispered something to Eddie, but none of us could hear the words.

Just as I suspected Eddie's head to come off, a wave of dark energy blasted us from behind. I stumbled back to the ground, landing on my hands and knees with Maciah right beside me.

Sam was nowhere to be seen, and I hoped that was a good thing for the she-wolf.

The normal white wisps of original power inside me were tinged with a murky grey color. I started with my arms and tried to expunge whatever it was, but no amount of shaking was breaking the dark energy loose from me.

Viktor was stalking toward us, his lips tilted up, but not quite smiling. His eyes were a dark crimson, and every step he made seemed calculated.

Maciah was struggling to stand, and I made it to my feet first, doing my best to help him just as he'd done for me, but every movement was more difficult than the last.

Viktor held his hand out, his eyes only staring at me. "My prize. Come join me."

I pulled the remaining potion from my chest and threw it at the vampire. Viktor moved out of the way, but

Beatrix was smarter than that. Her spell spread wide, and the impact of the small explosion rocked all of us.

I couldn't see where Viktor might have been hit, but that didn't matter. Whatever hold he'd had on us with his dark magic was broken, and that was a win for us.

CHAPTER 22

Once the smoke from the explosion settled, Viktor was nowhere to be seen, but neither was his dark energy, so I wasn't too nervous.

I grabbed Maciah's hand, drawing on our bond and focusing on my abilities. I had to be able to find Viktor, even if I couldn't see him.

The heaviness I'd been covered in only a minute before had completely dissipated, and my power shot out of me, desperate to get free—an action I hadn't experienced since before Beatrix did her juju on me.

"Are you okay?" Maciah demanded, but I held my hand up, silently asking him to give me a minute.

I could taste the sourness of Viktor's dark energy. He was close, but I couldn't tell what direction he'd gone. As I continued my search, using only my mind, I sensed that the bigger part of the fight had stayed at the house.

Vampires and wolves alike were still battling against each other.

Holden and some of his pack had stayed, but they seemed to be keeping to the outer parts of the battle, doing their best to make sure everyone was contained. A small, but impactful job we hadn't thought of.

"Is she okay?" I heard Rachel ask.

Maciah must have nodded and signaled for them to be quiet, because my concentration wasn't interrupted again.

I searched for another minute before snarling. "He's gone."

"What do you mean?" Maciah asked with a growl of his own.

"I mean his tainted energy is left behind, but I can't find him within a mile radius of this very spot." That fact pissed off every single one of us. We'd worked so hard to get him here, to set him up for a fight he didn't think we were prepared for.

I hadn't taken Viktor for a coward, but his lack of appearance was proving every predisposition I had about the old vampire wrong.

"Where's Nikki and Bennett?" Rachel asked.

I glanced behind us expecting to see them both there, but they weren't. Not even Eddie.

A wolf howled from the forest and my gut twisted. Something was wrong. I knew it as soon as the howl cut off and nobody came out of the trees.

I took a hesitant step forward with my crossbow

raised. There was movement beyond the shadows, but I couldn't tell what or who was there.

My skin burned with energy, my heart raced with dread, and the fight around us grew quieter by the second. Even still, I pressed my energy out once again, searching for our target. I found him. Only it was too late.

"No," Rachel cried out softly at the same time I saw them.

Viktor had Nikki and Bennett each held by their necks, both of them hanging limp and seemingly unconscious.

Viktor's beady red eyes met my hardened gaze. "You had a choice, Amersyn. You could have come to me willingly, but instead, you asked your friends to risk their lives in some feeble attempt to kill me. I tried to tell you before, but you didn't listen, and now they'll pay for your stubbornness."

Before any of us could move, Viktor tightened his hold on Nikki and Bennett until their bodies crumpled to the ground, separated from their heads. The deaths were quick and likely painless, given their slack forms.

My eyes cast to my feet for the briefest of seconds. I wasn't strong enough to watch them turn to ash. I couldn't. Not when Rachel wailed next to me and Maciah's pain soaked through me, overshadowing my own.

My throat burned with heightened emotions—a mix of grief, rage, and something I couldn't identify—as a white light grew within me. The wisps I'd always associated with my inherited power took a solid shape, pulsing inside me in time with the shifting of my emotions.

By the time I looked back up, Nikki and Bennett were officially gone, and Viktor was still standing at the tree line.

"Will you allow your other friends to find the same fate as these two, Amersyn? Or will you surrender yourself to me?" Viktor taunted, but the four of us had pushed beyond the shock and grief Viktor intentionally overwhelmed us with.

The shared wrath of Maciah, Zeke, Rachel, and myself swirled within each of us as we took a calculated step forward. No matter how hard this loss was going to hit, I knew none of us would let Nikki and Bennett's deaths be in vain.

Viktor would not best us. He wasn't going to take everything from me. Not a second time. Nikki and Bennett were the only wins that bastard would get, and he would pay for their lives dearly.

I charged for him with the others at my side, and renewed energy buzzed along my skin as I collided in the air with Viktor, doing something I probably should have tested first, but I was all out of cares to give.

With my energy coating my skin, I gathered as much of it as I could into my palm before slamming my hand against Viktor's chest, hoping to stun the bloodsucker before we took him down.

Maciah jerked me back before my feet touched the ground, but my eyes never left Viktor as the three of us crashed to the ground. I recovered quickly and pulled a stake from my hip, determined to send it through Viktor's chest.

The bastard rolled out of the way, and the stake lodged into the dirt instead of his heart. Viktor blurred left then right and left again before he launched himself at me.

I met him in the middle once again, my hands reaching for his neck. His fist connected with my stomach, sending me ten feet in the opposite direction, but Maciah was there to catch me while Rachel and Zeke used more of Beatrix's spells.

Explosion after explosion went off in front of us until we couldn't see Viktor, but I wasn't going to let him out of my sight. Not again.

"I'm sorry," I muttered to Maciah when I darted past him and into the cloud of smoke the potions had caused.

I couldn't see a thing, but my senses didn't rely on only sight. I listened for the vampire, knowing he had to have been hit by at least one of the potions. I searched for his mind, hoping to incapacitate him before my eyes found him.

A hand grabbed on to my ankle, and I kicked out, enjoying the crunching sound that followed the impact of my foot. I bent down, channeling my power through my arms and into my palms as my hands wrapped around Viktor's neck.

When I pulled him out of the smoke, he was smirking. "I'm going to take everything from you."

Little did I know, Zeke and Rachel were behind me and Viktor blasted them with dark energy that made me want to vomit as the bits of black magic floated over my skin toward their target.

I yanked Viktor's neck, throwing him toward the ground and pummeling my fist into his face. "You aren't taking anything else from me, you sick twisted bastard."

Viktor laughed in my face. "If I can't have my prize, then no one will."

His elbow came up and slammed into my left side, but I wasn't letting the bloodsucker go. We rolled together, and I caught sight of Maciah again as I ended up on my back.

My protector. He was right there, ready to act if I needed him, but not interfering with what I had to do. This was my fight to finish. Viktor was here because of me. He'd killed *my* family in search of me. I had to show him what a mistake he had made. I had to do this. Not on my own, but with the support of those I'd grown to love and trust.

Viktor grabbed hold of my shoulders, trying to pin me down, but I wasn't the weak little girl he'd been hunting all these years.

Maciah disappeared from my peripheral, hopefully going to Rachel and Zeke once he realized I was handling Viktor for the moment. In Maciah's place was a set of furious wolf eyes.

Sam leapt from the forest with her teeth bared and claws out. Her paw landed on Viktor's chest, ripping open his skin before she snapped her jaws, seeming to wait for my permission to end him.

Unfortunately, Viktor wasn't out of his tricks. Before I could consider giving Sam permission to rip the vampire's head off, Viktor reached for my arm and threw me behind him with little effort. By the time I got to my feet, he had Sam's wolf by the neck and was squeezing the life out of her, just as he'd done to Nikki and Bennett.

With a guttural roar, I charged at Viktor. I hardly knew Sam, but she was here fighting for us, and I wasn't going to let her die.

A wave of power left me just before my hand shoved into Sam's wolf in hopes of sending her soaring as far away from Viktor as possible. Maciah, Zeke, and Rachel were all headed my way, allowing my chest to release some of the tension I'd been holding in since Zeke and Rachel had taken the hit, but I couldn't focus on them for long.

With another stake in hand, I jammed the pointed tip into Viktor's chest. He flipped us around, throwing my aim off, and I ended up hitting his collarbone, but I wasn't done. Not even when I could feel his energy recharging, ready to strike me at a moment's notice.

As Viktor knocked us back to the ground, my hands reached up for his neck. He was hovering above me, and his dark magic crawled over my skin. Thankfully, I was prepared for that, letting my original power battle with the evil energy.

His lips parted, showing off his long fangs that were

ready to rip my throat out. "I'm going to kill you," he sneered, moving closer.

"Only in your dreams," I spat, gathering my own power.

With a force I didn't know I was capable of, I slammed one of my hands into Viktor's chest while the other stayed wrapped around his neck. I managed to knock him off balance before shoving the bastard onto his back. The impact rattled Viktor long enough for me to scramble on top of him, pinning him to the ground. I shoved my forearm against his throat as I pressed my other hand over his chest again.

He bucked underneath me, and my hold jostled, but Maciah, Zeke, and Rachel were right there with me, exactly when I needed them most. Maciah and Zeke each grabbed one of Viktor's arms as Rachel disappeared behind me, presumably grabbing his legs.

I kept one hand on his chest, using my power to keep him mostly immobile as I reached for another stake—the last one I hoped to need for the night.

My eyes met Viktor's cold ones. There wasn't a trace of fear or regret in them. He was a sick, murderous bastard through and through, but that stopped now.

"This is for my mother," I hissed as I pierced his chest with the stake, thankful my friends were keeping him still.

The last remnants of dark magic exploded from him, knocking each of us back, but the impact was nothing compared to what Viktor had been throwing around before. When I got to my feet, I was certain we'd won and that the battle was over, but there was no stake protruding from Viktor's chest as he rolled over to face me.

Mother-effing effer. Why wouldn't he just die?

He had only made it to his hands and knees by the time I shook off the heavy energy and blurred back to the vampire, not wasting a second on shock or fury. My hands grabbed on to his neck just as he'd done to our friends, and my nails cut into his skin with ease. He tried to throw himself backward, forcing me onto my back, but I was stronger, and I wasn't letting go of him. Not for any reason. Not even as I caught the sight of Sam's wolf prone on the ground and unmoving behind us.

With a ferocious scream, I squeezed harder on the bastard, uncaring about anything else until I removed his head from his neck.

Viktor was clawing at my arms, but I was done playing his games. I leaned forward and ripped a chunk of his neck out with my fangs before sinking my fingers into the injury while my other hand pressed down on his shoulder.

"Die, you son of a bitch!" With focused effort, his head finally tumbled off, but I didn't move away from the gore. My hold stayed on him until fissures formed along his body and ash scattered all around me.

I dropped to my knees, searching for Maciah, Zeke, Rachel, and Sam. My eyes spotted the wolf first. Her eyes were still unmoving, but her body was twitching as she fought against the remaining hold of Viktor's energy. Another wolf was racing toward her, so I moved on, looking for others.

Maciah's hand wrapped loosely around my ankle as he groaned. He was on the ground behind me, dark veins protruding from his neck.

My hands gently pulled him closer toward me. There was a large hole in his shirt where he'd been hit with Viktor's energy. The skin wasn't broken, but it was dark and angry and hot as I ran my fingers lightly over the marks that resembled char.

Maciah's breath stuttered, and then he went limp in my arms. He was no longer breathing or making a sound, but he also wasn't turning to ash, so hope wasn't lost. Not yet.

Zeke had his arm around Rachel as they hobbled together, kneeling beside me. "Is he…" Rachel tried to ask, but a sob cut off her words.

"I don't know," I said, stroking Maciah's head and frustrated that his wounds weren't healing. I couldn't lose him now. We'd won. We stopped Viktor. It was time for our peace. I couldn't have that without Maciah at my side.

"Maybe we can call Beatrix. She might not have wanted to fight, but she might be able to handle this," Zeke suggested.

"We don't have time for that." I didn't know how long we had, but the warmth I normally felt from Maciah was slipping away by the second and panic was beginning to choke me.

"What if you gave him some of your blood?" Zeke asked, and I was confused.

"What?"

"You're bonded. I could get blood from the house, but given the two of you have shared blood before, this might be better," Zeke explained.

It was worth a try. We'd only bitten each other twice, but the magical connection when we did was undeniable both times. Without wasting another second, I extended my fangs and used them to cut my wrist. Blood began to pool as I opened Maciah's lips.

Drips fell on his chest as I moved my arm toward him and positioned my wrist over his mouth. He wasn't actively feeding from me, and I hoped I wasn't going to make things worse by choking him.

With that thought, I used my other hand to angle his head up just to be sure.

"Look," Rachel said and pointed to his chest.

Smoke was rising, and as I swiped at the blood I trickled on him, the smoke cleared, as did the char marks on his chest.

"It's working," I said, tears filling my eyes in relief.

I switched hands when I felt my wrist begin to heal and opened the veins on the other one, placing it against Maciah's lips.

He groaned and began to jerk his body around, so I pulled my arm back and held his face tightly. "It's okay,

Maciah. You're okay. We're okay," I said softly until he settled, and his eyes began to flutter.

"Viktor...he..." Maciah muttered.

"I know, but he's dead now and you're going to be okay." My throat burned with emotion as my words registered with my heart.

We'd done it. Viktor was dead. But once again, the price of winning hadn't been cheap. We'd lost Nikki and Bennett, and I was sure there were others as well. Their lives would forever be remembered for what they sacrificed today.

My biggest hope was that Nikki and Bennett found each other again. They deserved that and so much more for their sacrifice.

Rachel and Zeke moved in closer, each of them wrapping an arm around us. We shared a moment of silence for our friends and a collective sigh of relief at the knowledge that Viktor couldn't take anyone else from us. Not now or ever again.

CHAPTER 23

Several hours later, morning came, but the rising sun brought no smiles. Lives had been lost. Hearts shattered. Worlds broken.

Losing Nikki and Bennett wasn't the only massive hit taken. Holden's wolves had lost two of their people while Sam's pack had Paul taken from them. He'd died taking a bullet that was meant for Collin, and judging by the look on Collin's sullen face, the wolf was wishing the roles had been reversed.

Sam nodded stiffly at Maciah and me. "We're going to head home. Thank you for the car."

Maciah had given her one of the vampire SUVs. "Burn it when you're done if you're so inclined," he replied.

"I just might," Sam said, but her normal attitude was missing from the words.

My gaze went back to Collin's bloodshot eyes. "Your loss will be remembered by us all."

He nodded. "Thank you."

Rich, the other shifter from their pack, dropped a hand on Collin's shoulder, guiding him toward the waiting vehicle.

Zeke and Rachel joined us, and Zeke went to Sam before she could get in the SUV. "Thank you, Samantha."

They embraced tightly as Rachel stayed by my side, holding my hand, tears brimming in each of our eyes.

Zeke was drying his face as Sam pulled back, turning away from us before we could see any emotion. We let her go without another word.

Rachel went back to Zeke, wrapping her arms around his waist.

I glanced around. There was nobody left except for the four of us once Sam, Collin, and Paul drove away.

Maciah had given Jazz, Gabe, and Nick the choice to stay or take some time off once the other vampires had dispersed. They'd chosen to go, and none of us blamed them. One of their own had turned against us, and we'd lost even more members of our nest.

It was a lot to process, and we all deserved to do so in our own way.

"What are we going to do now?" Zeke asked.

"We'll go home and start over. We did it once, and we'll do it again. Viktor won't take anything else away from us," Maciah said, voice full of strength, even though I knew his heart was crushed.

He'd only just gotten his friend back. Not only was

Bennett gone forever, but so was Nikki. A hard truth for all of us to accept.

"Where's home?" Rachel asked, a sob building in her throat before she barely got the two words out.

"Wherever we want it to be. As long as we're together," I answered, reaching for her hand.

EPILOGUE

The battle with Viktor had stayed with us long after it ended. Even though we had won, we'd lost so much—vampires and wolves alike. Rebuilding wasn't going to be easy, but we were doing our best to live the rest of our lives for those who no longer could.

As guilty as I felt at times, I knew that was what Nikki and Bennett would have wanted for us. Whenever my grief was at its highest, all I had to do was close my eyes and I could see Nikki's face clearly, glaring at me with her hands on her hips. "Don't waste this life or I'll come back just to kick your ass."

Some days I was tempted to take her up on that threat, but I didn't want the disappointment of her never showing to make the sorrow any worse, which was why we'd already began hunting again.

Maciah, Zeke, Rachel, and I picked up where I'd left

off back in Portland while we waited for the mansion to be rebuilt. The cabins were still usable, but we needed the main house finished to make it a proper nest before we started recruiting other vampires. Though, that didn't mean we couldn't hunt while we waited.

I wiped ash from my face and grinned at Maciah. "That was fun. And exactly what I needed tonight."

He shook his head at me. "Your version of fun is a lot different from most people."

"And your point would be…"

Maciah pulled me toward him as I slipped the stake into my back pocket. "No point. Just stating the obvious. Now, can we go home so I can strip you naked and wash all of this crap off of us?"

We'd killed four vampires that had been in town for the last two weeks, targeting human nightclubs and murdering nightly. They'd been hard to track, but I was relentless in my hunt to find them.

"Home sounds nice," I said as Maciah nipped at my shoulder.

"Just home?" Maciah murmured before slipping his hand over my ass.

I grinned. "Maybe the naked part, too."

"Right. Just maybe." He released his hold on me and blurred toward our new hunting vehicle, a blacked-out Range Rover. The one in LA had grown on Maciah, and he'd decided we needed one just like it once we came back to Portland.

Except ours had bulletproof glass and an armored body with roll bars inside and all the weapons a girl could ever need while slaying vampires.

I joined him at the vehicle where he was holding the passenger door open for me. Before I got in, I pinched his chin between my fingers. "I love you and can't wait to be naked in the shower with you."

He grinned. "I know."

"Cocky prick," I muttered under my breath as I slid into the seat.

Maciah ignored my comment and was in the driver's seat in the next second, but I hardly noticed as the adrenaline of the hunt began to wear off.

Rachel and Zeke had been helping us track the group, but they'd asked for the night off for some time alone and we had no problem with that. Maciah and I then turned the nightly hunt into a date of our own, trying to find some normalcy after all the hell we'd been through.

It wasn't until several weeks after we got home that I was able to go more than a day without tearing up over the loss of Nikki. Our womance would never be the same without her. Accepting that wasn't an easy feat.

Thankfully, Rachel, just being her amazing self, had captured photos of the three of us, and even Bennett once he'd made his reappearance. Those memories would be forever on our walls and cherished as we tried to move forward with our lives in their honor.

Given the mansion wasn't going to be move-in ready

for months, we'd moved into my old condo. At first, I'd been furious when Maciah asked if we could stay there—just the two of us—but after I yelled at him for trying to separate me from Rachel after all we'd been through, he kindly informed me that he'd bought the condo below mine for Rachel and Zeke to live in.

I wasn't sure how I'd gotten so lucky to have Maciah as mine, but not a day had passed since we killed Viktor that I didn't let him know how grateful I was.

Maciah drove to the condo and placed his hand over my eyes when he pulled into the parking garage. I tried to pull it away, but he pressed harder. "Wait a second. I have a surprise for you."

"I thought getting naked with you in the shower was the only thing I had to look forward to once we got home," I joked, trying to keep the mood light regardless of where my thoughts had been.

He didn't respond with words as he parked the Range Rover, but his enthusiasm and sexual need were equally palpable. "I'm going to pull my hand away, but promise me that you'll keep your eyes closed."

I nodded. "Promise."

There was an excitement in his voice that hadn't been there since before our home had been burned to a crisp, and especially since losing Nikki and Bennett. As much as I didn't like surprises, I couldn't fathom denying his request and ruining his fun.

Before I could think too long about what Maciah

might be up to, he was opening the door and unbuckling my seatbelt to lift me out of the seat. He carried me to the other side of the vehicle before setting me back on my feet and moving to my side.

"Okay, open your eyes," he said fervently.

I blinked several times as I tried to process what I was seeing. It was my car. My Lexus. The first just-for-me purchase.

The two-door hardtop had been special to me, but when it was totaled after asshole vampires ran me and Rachel off the road, I'd thought my baby was a goner, a demolished ball of steel never to be seen again.

I took hesitant steps toward the black beauty. "Is this the *same* one?" I asked breathlessly.

Maciah nodded, following me. "The one and only. Of course, you'd gone and splurged on a limited-edition car, so finding all of the parts to keep original to the way you'd had her built wasn't easy, but I wouldn't return her to you less than perfect."

My hands moved over the smooth surface of the roof. "You did this? For me?"

"Only for you," he replied softly.

I turned toward Maciah and leapt into his arms, holding his face between my hands. "Thank you."

"Your smile is thanks enough." His grip tightened on my ass. "Do you want to go for a ride?"

As much as I'd missed my car, there was a different type of ride that I was going to need first. "Maybe a little later," I murmured as I scraped my teeth over his neck.

Before I knew it, my back was pressed against the inside of the elevator, and the doors were closing behind us. "I'm not too proud to admit that was the answer I was hoping you'd give," Maciah said before kissing me.

I pulled back just enough to speak. "We have forever, and no one is ever going to take that from us."

"Forever doesn't seem like enough time to love you, but I won't take a single second for granted," Maciah whispered, his eyes darkening.

My legs squeezed tighter around his hips as the doors opened to our condo. "I love you."

"I love you, too, and I'm going to spend the rest of the night showing you just how much."

As he walked us into our bedroom, I couldn't stop the smile from growing on my face. Just a few months ago, I was trying to kill him in this very room.

Now, I was able to easily see the rest of our lives play out as he lay me on the bed, melting my insides with just one look.

I'd known the moment I'd laid eyes on Maciah that he would be different, and every day we had together made me more thankful than the day before.

Maciah was mine and I was his. There was nothing, and no one, that would ever change that. Not today or centuries from now.

Want to discuss all things Scorned by Blood and Mystics

and Mayhem? Join my reader group Heather Renee's Book Warriors!

Then, flip the page to see what's next for this world!

AFTERWORD

Mystics and Mayhem was a dream I had a couple years ago. It began with a snarky fae and turned into something I never predicted! If you're just joining us, Mystics and Mayhem is a fantasy world in which I've been writing the last few of my book series in.

None of the series contain spoilers to the others, only fun cameos from some of your favorite characters. If you want to start at the beginning, here is there recommended reading order:

Broken Court
Luna Marked
Scorned by Blood
Fated to the Wolf

If you've been around from the beginning, then I hope you're excited to see that there will be another series in this world! Fated to the Wolf will be a dual POV trilogy. The leading lady is a witch named Andie and do you remember that pesky rogue wolf named Foster that we've seen pop up a couple of times now? He's our brooding love interest. Don't tell the others...but he might be my favorite so far. That's a secret just between us, though!

Want to be the first to know when their story is out? Sign up for my newsletter and join my reader group for early sneak peeks and other updates! Options on the next page :)

Mostly, I just wanted to say thank you to my readers for embracing this world and all things Mystics and Mayhem! I've had a blast writing these characters and can't wait to see where else they take us!!

STAY IN TOUCH

Find Heather on Facebook:

Reader Group:

Want to talk all things books and get updates before anyone else? Come hang with me in my reader group!

Heather Renee's Book Warriors

Author Page:

Teaser and big updates are also posted here!

Heather Renee Author

Newsletter:

I send this out sporadically. Don't worry. You won't ever be spammed by me and you get a couple goodies when you sign up!

http://smarturl.it/HeatherReneeNL

ALSO BY HEATHER RENEE

Scorned by Blood

A complete New Adult Vampire series featuring a not-so-human leading lady and the sexy vampire bound to protect her no matter the cost.

Luna Marked

A complete New Adult wolf shifter series (dual POV) featuring a strong-willed leading lady and a patient, yet fierce alpha male.

Broken Court

A complete New Adult Urban Fantasy series featuring an unconventional and anti-heroine leading lady, a broody love interest, and a fae kingdom with a vile king.

Royal Fae Guardians

A complete Young Adult Urban Fantasy series featuring fae, magic users, a sweet romance, along with snark and humor.

Shadow Veil Academy

A complete Upper Young Adult Urban Fantasy Academy series featuring shifters, elves, witches, and more.

Elite Supernatural Trackers

A complete New Adult Urban Fantasy series featuring witches, demons, a smart-mouthed female lead, alpha males, and a snarky fairy sidekick.

Raven Point Pack Series

A complete Upper Young Adult Paranormal Romance series

featuring wolves, witches, vengeance, and fated mates.

Blood of the Sea Series

A complete Young Adult Paranormal Romance series featuring vampires, open seas adventures, and the occasional pirate.

Standalone

Marked Paradox - A complete Young Adult Fantasy fae story about a realm divided and one fae to bring them back together.

ABOUT THE AUTHOR

Heather Renee is a *USA Today* bestselling author who lives in Oregon. She writes urban fantasy and paranormal romance novels with a mixture of adventure, humor, and sass. Her love of reading eventually led to her passion for writing and giving the gift of escapism.

When Heather's not writing, she is spending time with her loving husband and beautiful daughter, going on their own adventures. For more ways to connect with her, visit www.HeatherReneeAuthor.com.